LOST

POWERTOOLS: THE SHIELDS, BOOK 2

JAYNE RYLON

HAPPY ENDINGS PUBLISHING

eBook ISBN: 978-1-947093-26-3

Print ISBN: 978-1-947093-27-0

Cover Design by Jayne Rylon

Editing by Mackenzie Walton

Proofreading by Fedora Chen

Formatting by Jayne Rylon

ABOUT THE BOOK

From New York Times and USA Today bestselling author Jayne Rylon comes a steamy new multi-partner series of interconnected standalone set in the Powertools universe.

As a medic for a team of do-gooder assassins, Kennedy usually patches up her partners after they've taken out some of humanity's trash.

This assignment is totally different. She's required to risk both body and soul to seduce her ex, Knox, and convince him to double-cross the cartel he's worked for since he left her without a backward glance.

Marcus has been addicted to Kennedy since they became partners at Shields. He can't turn away, even if it means watching her over their comms with the jerk who broke her heart and made her swear off relationships, including one with him.

When Marcus and Knox form an unlikely alliance, to keep a new superdrug from ruining more lives—like they destroyed Knox's—Kennedy is forced to make a decision:

continue to resist the potent chemistry they have together to protect herself or be brave enough to make up for the time all three of them have lost.

ADDITIONAL INFORMATION

Sign up for the Naughty News for contests, release updates, news, appearance information, sneak peek excerpts, reading-themed apparel deals, and more. www.jaynerylon.com/newsletter

Shop for autographed books, reading-themed apparel, goodies, and more www.jaynerylon.com/shop

A complete list of Jayne's books can be found at www.jaynerylon.com/books

For Lila Dubois

Thanks for putting up with me, for talking me off the ledge of author anxiety daily, for fighting Facebook on my behalf when they repeatedly and erroneously shut down my ad account, for being unafraid of looking stupid with me as we attempt to Tiktok, for always jumping right in and doing things when I would sit and think about them for a year first, and most importantly for over a decade of friendship.

You're my book bestie and my work wife. You can not escape, but I promise to always provide an ample supply of snacks!

PS. I intended to dedicate the last book to you but I effed it up so you get this one instead :)

1

Kennedy stepped into the hallway outside her apartment. The smell of new carpet and fresh paint reminded her the building was only weeks old, even though it already felt more like home than anyplace she'd lived before. She scanned her fingerprint and retina to lock the door behind her, then bumped into her neighbors doing the same outside their units. Marcus, looking finer than ever, was toweling off his chiseled torso and abs down to the waistband of his shorts. Diamond stud earrings glinted in the LED lighting along with the droplets he was swiping from his chest. Barefoot, it was clear he had settled in to the Shields headquarters as quickly as she had.

He grinned when he noticed she couldn't keep her appraising stare from traveling over his defined pecs and flat stomach to the trail of black hair, which dead ended at soft cotton. The remaining water danced with rainbows enhanced by the backdrop of his dark skin. By comparison, it made her very aware she couldn't so much as get a tan with her pasty complexion.

"Come on you two. You can flirt later," Sola called from the elevator bank where Aarav was holding the door open for her to enter. It would be easy to mistake him for a standup guy instead of a sniper when dressed in crisp black pants and a burgundy polo, his collar-length dark hair combed back, obscuring the usual waves in it, and his thick beard recently trimmed.

Sola, one of Kennedy's best friends and also her coworker, lived at the other end of the hall, next door to Aarav. The four of them worked closely together, and now they lived that way too. For people who did...what they did...cohesiveness could mean life or death in the field. It was also nice to have friends who wouldn't judge Kennedy for the twisted moral code she lived by since they did also.

Sola snapped her fingers, urging them to hurry. "Jordan sounded like he wasn't fucking around. It's not like him to get his briefs in a twist. Let's go."

Marcus's mouth flattened into a pinched line that couldn't detract from the lushness of his lips. "I'm hurrying. I was in the middle of showering after my workout. Trust me, I did you all a favor by slapping on some soap before getting out."

Despite the fact that he killed people for a living—they all did—he gestured for Kennedy to precede him as if he were a gentleman instead of an assassin. Or maybe he simply wanted to check out her ass.

Kennedy glanced over her shoulder. Yup, he was staring.

Truth be told, she didn't mind. Marcus had a way of making her feel desirable, even if she could never act on the attraction between them. They'd had their one oopsy, tipsy kiss last month during the grand opening of the Shields' new headquarters and the living areas perched on top of their work spaces and gym. She'd made it clear it could never happen again.

Despite how much she wished that wasn't so.

Marcus was a dangerous man. Lethal and kind. Worst of all, he gave her the illusion of safety, and the intense stares he often leveled at her never left a shred of doubt that their attraction was very mutual.

Tension zinged between the four of them on the ride to the ground floor, where their command center was nestled at the back of the unassuming security services office, which was a front for their more furtive operations.

When they entered the heart of the headquarters in downtown Middletown, James—their team manager—had already displayed a map, several bios, and a summary of their next case on the wrap-around screens that descended from the ceiling. Images of white bricks and an arsenal of guns made it pretty clear what they were dealing with.

Kennedy shuddered. Drugs. She hated these kinds of assignments. But on the other hand, as a doctor, she'd seen firsthand what that shit could do to people. Good people. Caring people. People she would have sworn loved her, even if it wasn't enough to keep them from chasing their next high.

Damn it.

"You okay?" Marcus asked, his head tipped slightly so she could see the wave pattern shaved into the sides of his hair. The number of times she'd imagined tracing those marks with the tip of her finger or maybe her tongue was obscene.

She focused on that instead of the nightmarish memories threatening to distract her when she could least afford it. "Of course."

Kennedy crossed her arms and took a seat at the colossal, glossy boardroom table, sinking into the buttery leather of whatever ergonomic chairs James had ordered for them. Jordan had spared no expense on their headquarters. Why should he? Being super spies willing to teeter on the edge of legality and take enormous risks paid incredibly well.

Marcus grabbed the place next to her. Sola plopped down on her other side, and Aarav sat beside Sola. Across from them were Nolan, James, Ransom, Levi, and two new guys who'd only been around a few weeks and were currently bunking together in one of the guest suites they'd incorporated into their facility. Plenty of room for the team to grow or for them to stash witnesses when they were on babysitting missions.

Liam, the blond walking refrigerator with an impeccably manicured beard, couldn't have been more different from his partner. A permanent five o'clock shadow hugged Ace's angular jaw and his jet-black hair had probably never seen a comb. Black-and-gray tattoos smothered every inch of his warm ivory skin. He practically vibrated with energy where Liam seemed calm enough that Kennedy might have to take his pulse to make sure he was still conscious.

Both men stuck close to Ruby. Kennedy wasn't sure if the woman was called that because it was her given name, because her hair was dyed a deep, unnatural red, or because the computer language moniker was a nod to her coding and hacking skills. The quirky geek girl had taken over all things cyber from her mentor, JRad, and quickly become a key member of their team. Not surprising when she came so highly recommended.

Regardless, the new recruits seemed to have formed

some sort of bond, even if Ruby was doing her best to ignore the way Liam and Ace edged closer to her at every opportunity.

Welcome to our world, kid. Kennedy exchanged a wry glance with Sola, who hid a smirk behind her hand before her gaze wandered to Aarav. Damn, they were all in trouble. This wasn't some silly reality show. They couldn't afford distractions.

Kennedy wondered what it was about their profession that seemed to lure in hordes of confident, capable, sexy men...and women. It might have been their willingness to put their lives on the line and do morally gray shit in order to make the world a better place in the big picture that attracted her to them.

Unconsciously, she peeked at Marcus. He peered a bit too casually straight ahead, making her certain he was watching her in his peripheral vision like he always seemed to do.

Before she could tell him to quit it, Jordan strode into the room. Dressed in black cargo pants and a matching turtleneck that hugged his lean, muscled torso, he took his place at the head of the table. Everyone sat a bit straighter when he glanced around at them, counting silently to make sure they were all in attendance before he began his briefing.

Satisfied, he started talking without wasting a second on pleasantries. "We've got a lead on a key informant from the Vipers and a narrow window to try to make contact with him."

"The Vipers?" Marcus asked. "As in one of the nastiest drug cartels on the planet?"

Jordan gave a single curt nod.

"I hope whoever tagged us on this is paying us extra."

Ransom pinched the bridge of his nose. "I met plenty of those bastards when I was locked up. They don't take kindly to people meddling in their business. None of the people we hunt do, but Vipers are next level."

Kennedy now understood Jordan's urgency and the heightened tension radiating from him. To anyone else, he'd seem unflappable. But each of the Shields on his team was trained to observe even the slightest change in demeanor and body language. Even though she was their medic, she had picked up plenty of tricks along the way. Their fearless leader was a bit too stiff when he rested his ankle on his opposite knee and knit his hands over his six-pack.

"They are." Jordan never revealed his sources, likely to try to protect his team. As a former government agent, he had plenty of customers who needed them to cut through red tape. "Think ten times our normal fee. It seems we've got a special connection to their guy. The agency who's hiring us to take care of this for them is hoping we'll be willing to exploit it. If we don't act fast, this chance will be *eliminated* and lost forever. They don't have time to run it through ten thousand channels or the proper incentive to get the mark to cooperate, I think."

Kennedy's eyes narrowed when Jordan flicked his gaze to her. As the team's medical support, her job was usually to hang back and patch up bullet wounds after the rest of their ragtag band of assassins did their thing. Maybe they were expecting to find a bunch of strung out victims for her to treat. She shuddered thinking of one of their prior assignments, which had left her administering Narcan as if she were passing out candy at Halloween.

Before Jordan could clarify what exactly he meant, he began rattling off details. Kennedy silenced her mind to focus on the information he shared. It could save someone's life, or cost it, when she needed to make split-second decisions in the field.

"One of our DEA liaisons tipped us off that there's a leak in the Vipers' organization." Jordan cleared his throat. "Someone told them where the next major shipment would be transiting."

"And you really think that's not a trap?" Nolan snorted.

"It already went down. Last night. And it wasn't bullshit." Jordan crossed his arms. "It was valid info. They shut it down and got critical leads on distributors as well as manufacturing locations."

"How much are they giving the rat?" Aarav wondered, his Bengali accent morphing the R into a purr. "Whatever it is, it isn't worth it."

"That's the thing. My contact doesn't get why he tipped them off. They didn't pay him. And it certainly isn't out of the kindness of his heart. But it's too good of an opportunity to waste, whatever his motive is."

"If the Vipers figure out who he is, that bastard is going to regret his life decisions." Marcus shook his head. "Idiot. Those kinds of risks are only worth it for enough money to be set for life, and only if you have a damn good hiding place to hunker down in and never show your face again. I'm surprised they didn't slaughter the entire gang to make sure they fixed the problem permanently."

None of the Shields could argue with that. After all, Jordan paid each of them a fortune to be sitting there right then, and to be doing...whatever it was he was about to ask of them later.

Kennedy couldn't help the dread coating her guts like a bad infestation of *clostridium difficile*. Was it her imagination, or did Jordan keep peering in her direction disproportionally to the rest of the team? What the hell?

Marcus shifted, edging his chair closer to her. As much as Kennedy hated to admit it, she didn't mind his nearness or the instincts that scooted him slightly in front of her. They'd plunged themselves into plenty of hazardous situations together and he'd always taken care of both of them, protecting her as she tended to the wounded.

Kennedy had come to trust him, at least in the field. And for her, that was kind of a miracle.

"You said this Viper is connected to us...how?" Levi asked. "It's not someone Ransom knew in jail, is it?" His fingers twitched on the arm of his chair. For a Shield, especially a former undercover agent like Levi, that was about as drastic a tell as if he'd thrown himself around his partner and lover. The man he shared with their wife, Sevan.

Jordan let Levi off the hook. "No."

Levi swallowed and avoided Ransom's glare, the one that promised they'd be having a discussion later about being able to handle themselves and how their relationship couldn't interfere with work. It was one Kennedy had heard them have before, sometimes with raised voices. Yet another reason she could never do all the things to Marcus while she was awake that she'd dreamed of doing to him while she slept.

It would be far too complicated. Too messy. Not worth it.

She peeked at his strong jaw and his gorgeous brown eyes, flecked with gold.

"This is going to be a task that's handled best with a gentle touch..." Jordan cleared his throat and everyone shifted their attention to Sola, who twirled one long strand of her dark hair around her finger and grinned.

"Who am I sleeping with this time? Is he hot at least?" She made a hell of a seductress, and never seemed to mind the role, either. It was a highly effective persuasion and distraction technique. They didn't use it often, but when it was most expedient and reduced the risk to the other agents, she never hesitated to employ whatever skills she had to get the job done.

Aarav on the other hand, glowered.

"Not you." Jordan shook his head. "Not this time."

"Ah, damn. Is our Viper into guys?" Sola sighed dramatically. "I have a strap-on. I could wear a disguise."

"I told you, Jordan… Now that I'm with Laurel and Jace, I can't work those sorts of jobs anymore. I would never cheat on them or risk their health. Especially not with their history. Intimacy is something we only share with each other." Nolan winced. He'd done nearly as well as Sola when they needed super-spy peen as bait instead of pussy.

"Not you either." Jordan waved off Nolan's objections. He winged his laser stare to Kennedy and said, "You're the best candidate for this position."

"Me?" she squeaked at the same time Marcus grumbled, "No way."

Which of course made Kennedy swallow any objections she might have had in favor of shooting daggers at her neighbor. "Why the hell not? Maybe he's into blondes. He wouldn't be the only guy I know who is."

Marcus snapped his mouth closed. Neither of them could deny the passion with which he'd kissed her in this very room not so long ago. Not that he'd admit it in front of their boss and co-workers. Damn straight.

"I believe you know our target." Jordan cleared his throat then nodded to James, who displayed a picture on the giant screen.

Kennedy's breath left her lungs in a whoosh and she doubled over as if someone had punched her in the stomach. The hardened face, the tattoos, the broad shoulders and cut muscles—those were all new. But those eyes. She would never forget those eyes as long as she lived.

"Knox?" Her response sounded strangled even to herself. She couldn't believe she'd uttered his name nearly ten years after swearing to forget it. Forget him. Forget the wounds he'd inflicted that had long since scarred over.

Then suddenly she was laughing, maybe a bit hysterically. She swiped a tear from the corner of one eye, hoping her teammates thought it was from her cackling and not the bittersweet memories that rushed her at the sight of his world-weary expression.

Sola leaned in. She put her hand on Kennedy's shoulder and murmured, "You don't have to do this. It's not as easy as I make it seem sometimes. Especially if you have a history with this dude."

Kennedy winged a glance at Marcus, who stewed.

It was the dead last thing she should do in the world, but she found herself saying, "I don't know why you think this is going to work, Jordan. Knox left me without a look back. He loves drugs more than anything and I can't imagine that's gotten any better hanging around the Vipers for the past ten years."

Marcus snarled under his breath, "Fucking dumbass."

"He's sick." Kennedy whipped her stare to him. The problem had been that she hadn't been able to cure him. Not then and she wouldn't be able to now no matter how much training she had. That wasn't what they were asking of her, though. They were only requesting she help keep him alive long enough so he could in turn provide information that would save hundreds or thousands of others.

Son of a bitch.

"I understand," Jordan's quiet compassion was almost harder to bear than Marcus's righteous anger. "But you're our best shot. And Ransom is right—these guys don't fuck around. He's on borrowed time. Try to persuade him, however necessary, to come here with you and cooperate with us. If all else fails, we need you to distract him long enough that we can take him into protective custody and go from there."

So it was either seduce him and risk breaking herself, or don't and watch him die.

It was no choice at all. Hell, she'd regretted nearly half her life not being able to save him the first time around. Maybe she could at least have a second chance at that. There wasn't a single waver left in her voice when she confirmed, loud enough for everyone in the room to clearly hear, "I'm in."

"Thank you." Jordan relaxed ever so slightly. "And if you change your mind, tell me. We'll figure something else out."

Marcus stared at her, but she shook her head. She wasn't going to back out. Not because she felt pressured, but because a part of her she didn't want to acknowledge was more excited than it should be about her latest assignment.

She hated Knox. But she loved him too. Even after all this time and how thoroughly he'd shattered her heart.

2

Knox gripped the shot glass. He raised it to his lips and grimaced as the astringent aroma assaulted his nostrils. Had he really ever done this for fun?

Nah. Truth was, he'd done it to get numb, but neither drugs nor alcohol had ever entirely chased away his suffering in the moment. Plus, they'd only made his agony far worse in the long run. And now here he was, utterly ruined. He'd thought the night he'd OD'd along with Riggs—the one where only he'd pulled through—had been rock bottom, but he'd unfortunately survived that one without his best friend and sometimes fuck buddy. Now he had a feeling he'd seen the sun for the last time.

Did he really want to go out sober and completely aware?

Knox set the drink back down, glanced around the room, then snarled a curse. His life was so fucked up, a series of bad decisions, that one more shot wasn't going to make it worse. It might mute some of the anxious thoughts screaming at him in competition with the crappy country music blaring in the rundown honkytonk he was sitting in.

Despite lurking in the middle of some backwoods swamp, the Vipers would find him. They were probably slithering through the long grass outside on their way to ambush him right then. There was nowhere he could run they wouldn't look eventually. It'd be better if he wasn't too alert when they caught up with him.

Cheap whiskey set his throat on fire as it absorbed into his gullet. It disguised the acid churning there at the thought of the dead end he'd backed his dumb ass into. The Vipers weren't the sort of organization that would accept a resignation letter. He knew too much...had *done* too much for them to ever let him simply walk away.

But neither could he bring himself to sell the shit they'd given him, which was right now sitting unattended in the cabin he'd rented out back. Twenty-five pounds of some new hyper-opioid worth over a million bucks. Ordinarily he'd have subcontracted a whole team for security. Would have tested the dope himself several times to make sure it was as good as they said. Instead, all he could see when he looked at those bricks were Riggs's dead eyes staring up at him. Hell, he'd even had nightmares about Kennedy again since quitting cold turkey, her well-deserved disappointment in him slicing his soul. Maybe that's why he'd chosen this dump, the secret hangout they'd found when they'd been young and he liked to party while underage. She'd never hit the bar with him, but she'd danced far past her curfew with him. That seemed like a lifetime ago.

Funny how things changed when you didn't give a shit anymore.

Knox had gone rogue, in more ways than one. And

despite the fact that he had been an outlaw long enough to be trusted by one of the world's most nefarious cartels, there were consequences when that loyalty so much as wavered, never mind disintegrated. As soon as they realized it had been him who had tipped off the cops, there would be swift justice. His seconds were slipping away.

So, basically, this was his last drink. For real this time. No matter how often he'd sworn the same, pretended like he might be able to get his demons under control and right some of his wrongs, this was it. He was done. Hopefully, a slight buzz—stronger than he would have thought after barely a sip, probably because he'd abstained from drinking and drugs for a few months— would dull the pain when someone, whoever the Vipers sent to do the job, took him out.

He looked over his shoulder for the five-thousandth time that hour. Hell, he was shocked they hadn't done it last week, right after he'd "spilled" a few strategic secrets to that dude he'd damn well known was an undercover agent of some sort.

Knox could only hope his too-late change of heart had saved a life or two. It wouldn't make up for all the shit he'd done wrong, but it would be nice to go out knowing he'd refrained from doing any more harm. In fact, maybe he could feed some of his delivery to the inky black waters out back before they caught up with him. It probably wouldn't save his soul, but it was the least he could do.

His mind made up, Knox grimaced, then stood too fast. His bar stool rocked. It would have toppled, but a slender, pale hand tipped with trim, pink nails reached out to catch it.

"Thanks," he mumbled. But when he looked up, the

whole universe tilted. And it had nothing to do with the shot he'd downed either. The absolute last person he expected to see stood right in front of him. And that's when he was certain he was worse off than he'd realized. Because there was no chance in hell it was a coincidence she reappeared in his life during its final hours.

"Kennedy?" He groaned. "What the hell are you doing here?"

Knox reached behind himself for the bar. Because if Riggs had been one of his biggest regrets, the only one that could top it was right there in front of him, like the ghost of all his past mistakes, staring straight into his soul with neon-blue eyes that hadn't dimmed one damn bit since he'd last gazed lovingly into them, begging her to understand that he wasn't as strong as she'd given him credit for.

Knox wished he'd slammed the whole bottle instead of one measly shot.

3

———————

Kennedy attempted to ignore the wave of lust that crashed over her at the sound of her name falling from Knox's lips. It had been years since she'd heard that sound in person, but only hours since it had echoed through her dreams.

Though she'd played it cool with Jordan and the rest of the Shields, Marcus especially, there was nothing blasé about her attitude toward the man in front of her now. He was no longer the boy she'd grown up with, his once-smooth skin dotted with facial hair and his barely-there laugh lines now etched into grooves that only came with time and persistent anxiety.

At least she wouldn't have to pretend to be attracted to him. Because as much as she'd loved the boy he'd been, her body responded instinctively to the man he'd grown into. And if his hard edges turned her on despite the unfortunate reality of how he'd earned them, well, she'd talk to the team's shrink about that in her next session. For this one night, she had a free pass.

She could experience everything she'd regretted not

doing with him before and pretend it was for the greater good instead of her own personal needs. It was a perfect out, if that's what it took to either persuade him to come back to Shields with her or to distract him so that they could force him to.

Kennedy made her brain replay what he'd just asked so the gap before her response didn't grow too long and awkward.

"What am I doing here? Same as you, I suppose." She shrugged as if she hung out in dive bars and took men home for meaningless fucks all the time when in fact she hadn't been to this shithole or any other since the last time they'd partied there together. "Grabbing a drink and maybe someone to spend the evening with. Maybe I was feeling nostalgic."

"Really? Holy. Fucking. Shit." He shook his head as if he couldn't believe it.

And she didn't blame him.

Nothing could be further from the truth. No, her nights were usually spent supporting her friends as they ended bad guys, and patching them up when shit went weird. Or hanging out with them at the Shields' headquarters, planning, plotting, exercising, or lately falling asleep on Marcus's couch after watching movies with a solid two-cushion-width safety zone between them.

Who would provide medical assistance for her if things didn't go according to plan today?

Kennedy forced those thoughts from her mind as Knox scrutinized her reaction. He was no idiot, but if he doubted her story, he didn't call her on it. Instead he leaned against the bar as if he needed it to steady him. Great, exactly how much had he had to drink? James had told her he'd only ordered one, though he could have frontloaded before arriving. Or maybe he was on something else. Something harder.

Kennedy's stomach cramped.

"You okay?" Knox asked, making her aware that she'd winced and pressed her hand to her middle. Why did he still have the power to turn her insides to mush at the slightest show of affection or concern? He reached out as if to steady her when they both knew he was the one who'd always been on shaky ground.

"Yeah, I'm fine. Just kind of a shock to see you again."

"Still get those nervous poops like before big tests, huh?" Knox barked out a laugh. "You should see a doctor about that."

"I *am* a doctor." She didn't see any reason to lie about that.

"No shit." Knox seemed impressed but not entirely surprised. He'd always told her she could be whatever she chose.

"Yeah, what about you?" she asked, although she already knew the answer. He was a bad guy. The kind of person they hunted. One who'd been lured into things he likely would never have considered, never mind done, if it weren't for the draw of drugs. Except, when she peered into his eyes, she saw a glimmer of the person he'd been and wondered if he could really be trying to find himself as desperately as she once had.

"I'm a loser." He would have turned away then, but she stopped him with her hand on his shoulder.

"You know I never thought that about you." An addict, yes. A horrible human being, of course not. Addiction did awful things to a person.

"Well, I always said you were a terrible judge of character," Knox spit out.

"I guess I still make bad decisions sometimes then." She forced out an ironic laugh at the end of her deliberately seductive innuendo. It was the truth, he just had no idea how true it was. This whole op was going to give her nightmares for the next ten years to rival the ones she'd lived with for the past decade. But how could she have said no? Maybe she'd been granted one last chance to save him. Them?

Kennedy swallowed hard.

"What the hell does that mean?" Knox's gaze snapped to hers.

"Want to make one with me? Poor judgment loves company." She rocked forward so that she whisper-shouted the question a fraction of an inch from his too-familiar lips. Already, she could imagine what they would taste like: sin and crappy whiskey.

"What exactly are you asking?"

"I'm saying, if you're of sound mind to make these sorts of decisions…"

"I've only had one damn drink," he grumbled. "Should have had another."

"Nothing else?"

He shook his head, grimacing, and she felt comfortable he was sober enough to give his consent.

"Then let's get out of here and go somewhere we can actually hear each other when we talk. Catch up. Or just pick up where we left off and skip all that other bullshit, huh?" Kennedy ignored the incredulous stare Knox shot her as she slapped a twenty on the bar and jerked her chin toward Liam, the "bartender," who nodded, confirming the team had finished their part while she chatted with her mark. Aarav had helped Marcus and Sola wire Knox's bunk with all sorts of surveillance devices she didn't want to think about.

Because the truth was, she might play it off like she was taking one for the team by hooking up with Knox—while the rest of the Shields watched and listened in both for her safety and for leverage—but the truth was she would be living out one of her fantasies, to have one more chance to be close to her puppy love and pray that he might make a different decision at this juncture in their lives.

Now *that* was stupid. This was only going to end one way—with him hating her as much as she had pretended to despise him while nursing her broken heart.

"I've got a cabin out back." Knox tipped his head as he squinted at her, as if trying to evaluate if she was really serious. She didn't blame him. The old her never would have been this bold. Hell, today her wouldn't have been without the Shields' directive either.

Kennedy channeled Sola, wishing she was as brazen as her friend, then curled her finger with the fresh polish the other woman had applied for her, and strutted toward the door, pretending to be a lot more confident than she felt.

Only the vibration of Knox's heavy booted steps behind her, and James's intel—whispered into the earpiece he'd assured her was invisible to the naked eye—calmed her doubts and fears. "He's on your ass like Nolan's truck was on the bumper of my poor little car."

"I told you, it's too small to see." Nolan had apologized a million times already.

"No one's ever complained about my size before," James huffed.

Kennedy knew they were being lighthearted during

the op for her benefit. Usually it was radio silence and precision, but they needed her to act natural, relaxed, or Knox would never fall into her trap. She wasn't a superspy like Marcus or Jordan or Sola. She was a doctor, damn it.

But just this once, the team needed her. And she wasn't going to let them down.

Hell, maybe even she had to win some closure for herself.

On the way out, she spotted Nolan leaning up against one of the porch posts on the rickety deck. He appeared to be far more interested in the woman he was chatting up than her, but she knew he was reading the situation from Sola's expression as easily as a reflection of her and Knox when they passed by.

Kennedy wasn't alone with Knox. That was both a relief and horrific.

Because Marcus was somewhere out there in the woods. And he could hear every damn word they said. Could he also catch the way her breathing had grown shallow and fast just knowing Knox was right there, within arms' reach, and that what they were about to do next...maybe...hopefully...was going to be a hell of a lot more intimate than rehashing bad memories.

Knox caught up to her pretty damn quick, his longer strides making it easy for him to rest his fingers on her elbow as if he had every right to guide her deeper into the pretty green trees dripping moss. As the music faded, and the sound of rustling branches and birds or other small animals sprinting away from them in the underbrush on either side of the path became more prevalent, the pounding of her heart threatened to drown out her thoughts.

Thankfully, neither of them broke the temporary

serenity until he slid a key from the pocket of his ripped jeans, unlocked the door, and ushered her inside.

James alerted the rest of the team to shift to their secondary positions. "Places, Shields. They're in."

And now it was entirely up to her. Could she get Knox to come peacefully? Anything else carried a threat, however minor, to the health and safety of her team, to Knox, and to herself.

She wasn't sure how to broach the subject. Thankfully, he was a man of action.

If his vanishing act ten years ago had made her doubt the attraction she'd thought arced between them, he at least erased any doubt from her mind when he pinned her up against the wall barely inside the door, pushed his knee between hers and leaned in so that she felt every inch of him, from his shoulders to his thigh against her pussy, and his hard cock in between.

Unbidden, a sigh escaped her parted lips. His eyes dilated and he closed any remaining gap between them, laying his lips over hers and kissing the shit out of her.

A barely audible growl echoed across the otherwise silent comms. The fact that she knew it was Marcus's and that he might be a tiny bit jealous didn't make what Knox was doing to her feel any worse. She was probably going to go to hell for this, but at least she was sure she was going to enjoy it first.

4

Kennedy took some solace in the fact that it hadn't required any seduction on her part to land her in Knox's bed. Well, okay, in his arms. Because at the rate they were going they might not even make it to the frumpy quilt-covered mattress bracketed by an outdated brass-bar head and footboard over in the corner of the cabin.

Knox's urgency was tinged with desperation. It salved the part of her that had never recovered from him so easily walking away from what they'd had. It also let her conscience off the hook, because she felt like she hadn't coerced him into doing something he wasn't interested in. That was doubly important when she was about to betray him as he'd done to her so many years ago.

"Stop thinking so much." Knox rasped before nipping her neck, right below her ear. "For once in your life, just feel. Live in the moment."

Damn, the reverberations of his primal touch shot through her body, straight to her toes, which curled in her boots. As much as she kept trying to convince herself she was sacrificing her better sense for the Shields, she couldn't help but melt a little inside as she stared straight into Knox's emerald eyes. His face, his body, his soul— every bit of that had changed, hardened. But his eyes were so familiar they threatened to break her.

Kennedy reached for Knox, tunneling her hands into the sides of his reddish hair, remembering how silky smooth it felt running between her fingers. It was shorter these days, neater, but still as soft. The only part of him she could say that about.

His arms were like steel as they bracketed her, his forearms planted from elbow to wrist on either side of her shoulders before he leaned on one and put the other to good use. He caressed the entire length of her arm, which was bared in the candy-pink tank top she wore, before briefly squeezing her hand.

And as he did, his lips brushed hers. Both of them gasped before he bounced back, this time sealing their mouths completely. Instinct took over from logic as she surrendered, allowing him access to her entire being when she should have been guarding herself from the influence he obviously still held over her body and, likely, her emotions.

There would be plenty of time to kick herself for this later. So she might as well make it count while she could. Kennedy slid her hands lower so they cupped his neck and used the grip to keep him close and devour him even as he did the same to her.

Knox leaned in, his thigh nudging her pussy, making her rub up against him in a sinuous motion she didn't know she was capable of until her body craved more.

With each kiss he erased a year of the time they'd spent apart. They might be strangers now, but her body recognized his and remembered their teenaged make out sessions. This time she didn't intend to stop without having all of him. Kisses and heavy petting weren't going to be enough to put out the fire he lit inside her as if she'd been kindling drying out without him.

"You smell so good. Clean." He inhaled, his nose buried in her hair as he caught his breath. His parted lips brushed the skin of her neck as he murmured to her, "I've never forgotten that."

Knox had grown up in shitty circumstances. His mom had been a kid herself when she'd had him. Passed around to relatives who had too many of their own mouths to feed to keep him off the streets for long, Knox had fallen through the cracks. He'd always been obsessed with basics she took for granted, like the concept of leftovers or freshly shampooed hair, and it seemed that hadn't changed. So why hadn't he taken the chance he'd had to alter the path his life was on? Why had he thrown it all away—her love included—and gone right back to the gutter he'd nearly clawed his way out of?

She knew the answer, but as someone who'd never experienced addiction, it was still sometimes impossible for her to wrap her head around it.

Then again, she'd never had sex with a man before either and here she was, completely sure of how to react to the things he was doing to her body despite her lack of previous real-life exposure to those stimuli.

Kennedy put her extensive knowledge of anatomy to good use. She shoved her hand under the faded T-shirt that hugged his ripped torso and ran her thumbs along the ridge formed by the tendon that stretched from his iliac crest toward his groin, fashioning a delicious V pointing straight to his cock. Then she worked upward, bunching the thin cotton of his shirt in her hands as the backs of her knuckles skimmed his washboard abs. Damn. He might have been underweight but his lack of body fat put all of him on display.

It didn't take long before she whipped the fabric from him, his hands halting their roaming only long enough for her to rid him of the shirt. He didn't even bother to kick off his boots before unbuttoning and unzipping his pants.

She breathed a sigh of relief. Hopefully he wouldn't bother taking the time to fully undress her, because being naked with him would have made her feel too vulnerable. Even if she was a physician and had seen more bodies than she could count, exposing herself to someone else—him especially—wasn't something she was good at...or had much practice with.

In that moment, she imagined what it would be like if she'd given in to the equally as strong attraction between her and Marcus any of the times they'd had the opportunity to be intimate. She couldn't imagine him ever settling for something this perfunctory. No, Marcus would be the kind of man to savor every stitch he removed from her and delight her with hours of foreplay before he ever gave in to his own desires. He was a legend, a man built from patience.

She shuddered, wondering what it would be like to have the best of both worlds—Knox's passion and Marcus's thoroughness. Hey, why not? Lots of her friends had committed poly relationships.

Besides, thinking of Marcus now, knowing he was practically there right on the other side of the comms and somewhere outside in the scrub, made her so much more secure and confident as she took this wild leap. She hoped all the porn she'd watched and nights spent with her arsenal of toys, pleasuring herself, would be enough to make her attempts at fucking Knox less laughable. Hell, he'd already had more experience at fifteen than she had now closing in on thirty.

She figured she wasn't going to have to worry about much except letting him take the lead when he leveled her with the most intense stare she'd ever seen and shoved his hands under her skirt. His fingers wrapped around the lace of her panties. "You don't care if I destroy these, do you?"

She gulped and shook her head no.

He ripped her panties from her and had her hoisted over his shoulder before she could fully register his intent. His broad palm on her ass kept her securely in place as he marched the three short steps to the bed.

He tossed her onto it, the metal frame creaking ominously as she bounced, then followed her. Except this time he didn't stop at kissing her. Sure, that's where he started, his tongue swiping along hers before he yanked her tank top down so that her breasts, small enough not to require a bra, were exposed, smooshed up and together by the cotton of her shirt.

He took a second or two to fondle and suck on them before slithering between her legs. His head disappeared beneath her skirt and then she nearly forgot to think, forgot why she was there, and that this wasn't just another lascivious dream of hers that he was starring in. No, that was his tongue, exploring every fold of her labia before doing something none of her toys had ever come close to simulating on her flesh.

She moaned and writhed beneath him, trying to press herself tighter to his face when that would have been impossible. Around the time he pressed two fingers deep inside her, Kennedy knew it wouldn't take much more for her to shatter. She tried to stifle her wild cries, fully aware the entire team—and one man in particular —could hear every catch of her breath, whimper, and moan.

But it was no use. Knox was as good at pleasuring her as she'd always imagined he would be.

"So sweet," he growled against her. "Going to be heaven on my cock."

Kennedy blinked back to reality. Right. This wasn't about her. Shit. "Then fuck me."

"Not until you're ready." He redoubled his efforts, making her quiver around him.

"Been waiting for half my life. No more." And although it was the truth, she regretted not being able to linger, to fully savor the moment. This certainly wasn't how she'd ever imagined losing her virginity. Though she'd be lying if she said she wasn't thrilled it would finally be out of the way, a mental obstacle removed. Maybe if she could view sex like Sola or some of her other friends did—a casual physical relief—she wouldn't be so damn lonely or anxious about sharing intimacy with someone she wasn't in love with anymore.

Maybe Marcus...

Kennedy shook herself when Knox groaned and rose up over her. He ripped open his jeans and shoved them halfway to his knees. Still wearing them and his boots, he covered her. The thick length of his shaft settled between her legs, her skirt the only thing separating them.

Kennedy was a doctor. She knew damn well Knox had probably taken chances with his health. Maybe even shared needles with people. She lunged for the purse she'd dropped on the floor in the thankfully tiny room and took out a condom, handing it to him.

"You always carry those?" One of his scarred brows rose.

"I'm a responsible adult, yes." She silently dared him to make some stupid comment about it. So what if she'd gotten them fresh from the store on her way to this meet up? She could hook up with whomever she damn well pleased. The last thing she planned to do was let him know that he'd ruined her for relationships with anyone else, made it impossible for her to open up to men in general, and one specific guy in particular.

Marcus. Kennedy bit her cheek to keep from wincing. At least she wouldn't have to worry about resisting temptation around him anymore. After this assignment he probably wasn't going to be interested in her anymore. The loss she felt at that threatened to distract her from Knox ripping open the condom and rolling it down his thick shaft.

In that moment, she realized how unfair she'd been to both herself and her partner. She respected Marcus, desired him, and had smothered those feelings because she'd been afraid.

Son of a bitch. This was not the time for revelations.

"Second thoughts?" Knox asked her.

Sola jumped in over the comms. "Bail if you're not one-hundred percent. We've got the cabin surrounded. We'll get him one way or another."

It shocked her when Marcus whispered into her ear while the rest of the team—Jordan and James especially, who both usually directed their missions—was dead silent. "Don't let him out. Not yet. You've almost got him. He could take you hostage, hurt you before we could get to him. And it sounds like you're having fun. Go ahead, Kennedy. Enjoy yourself. It's win-win. If you can tie him up like we talked about, even better."

So he didn't care that she fucked her ex if it meant capturing him peacefully?

Kennedy wasn't sure if she was thrilled or utterly discouraged by that.

Still, she couldn't deny that Marcus was right. That's why they'd formulated this plan in the first place. It was better to do this without resistance. Maybe after she wrung Knox dry he'd be too chill to put up a fight. For the sake of her friends and for him, she wanted to do this the easy way.

Kennedy ignored the Shields and responded to Knox. "Nope."

She took his sheathed cock in hand and aimed it between her legs.

"Good. Because I'd like to have at least one thing I never thought possible before I die. I don't deserve this, but I'm going to take it anyway because we both know I'm selfish as fuck."

Knox blanketed her, shoving up her skirt and fitting the blunt head of his cock to her opening. Kennedy held her breath and spread her legs wider to accommodate his hips between her thighs. He settled in, fusing them an inch or so before pausing to make sure she was okay.

It was different than she'd expected. He was warm and a little softer than some of her toys, though plenty stiff to get the job done. One taste was enough to know she wanted everything he could feed her.

He might still believe—as he had when they were young—that he was a terrible person, unworthy of all the things she'd wanted to share with him, but just like then, she saw the hints of the man he truly was...or could be... glimmering beneath his street life surface.

"Good?" he asked though his jaw twitched with the effort of holding himself in check.

Kennedy would have said yes regardless, but she was shocked when she let herself focus on the pleasure that radiated from where they were joined, her body accommodating him with only the perfect amount of delicious ache. She nodded, then reached around to grab his ass and drag him closer. Thankfully, time and her toys had done away with whatever might have remained of her hymen and he seemed to have no clue he was in uncharted territory.

Knox cursed, then sank inside her, wedging his cock into her and opening her to her first taste of a man within her. It was glorious. Relief—both physical and mental—coupled with ecstasy, making her shudder as he worked fully within her.

"You're everything I always imagined you would be," he murmured before kissing her sweetly.

Oh hell, no. That would not do. She had given him her body, but there was no way she would let him steal her heart again.

Kennedy shoved one of his shoulders and rolled hard to that side. She wound up perched on top of him. His cock speared impossibly deeper as she planted her hands on his chest and began to grind on him. His eyes blazed as he watched her take control, and to her surprise, he didn't try to wrest it back from her.

He let her use him, pleasure herself with his body, and lifted his hands to the bars of the headboard, holding on as if to keep himself from reaching for her and stopping the display of power she hadn't realized she was capable of.

In that moment, she knew she had Knox. She snatched her purse from where she'd dropped it on the bed beside him and used the long leather shoulder strap to bind his wrists and hands to the headboard. He thrashed but didn't come free, then sagged, resigned.

"Didn't realize you were into that." He grinned up at her, his stiff cock buried inside her proof that he didn't mind in the least.

"Me either." She shrugged then rocked, her body refusing to settle now that she'd riled it beyond the point of no return. Kennedy rose and fell over him, grinding on him so that her clit rubbed against the flat pad of muscle above his cock.

It only took three strokes before her entire body exploded around him. Whether from the taboo nature of fucking him while her teammates observed them, the lifelong fantasy of having him to herself come true, or the fact that she'd never gotten to experience this carnal pleasure with anyone before, it all came to a head in one sonic boom of rapture.

"Yes. Hell yes. Come on me, Kennedy. You're so fucking tight milking my cock like that. Now untie me so I can fuck you right," Knox growled.

"You have him bound?" James asked then.

"Yes," Kennedy panted, but not to Knox. She was talking to James. Which became apparent when she gave them more explicit directions. "We're good. Come and get him."

"Wow. Seriously?" Knox blinked a few times then yanked at his bonds, still unable to break free. "I didn't think you had it in you to go through with it. My bad for underestimating you."

Kennedy didn't bother to respond when they both apparently knew she'd betrayed him and everything was happening so fast. Her body still rang with the reverberations of her climax and they only had seconds before the Shields swarmed the room.

She pressed her hand to the side of her head, hoping to mute her comms or muffle them at least. "You didn't come with me?"

"Was going to make sure you had more than one lousy orgasm first. Give me some fucking credit." Knox grimaced, his erection twitching within her, setting off aftershocks. He smiled sadly up at her, breaking her heart all over again. "I'm glad you enjoyed yourself, but you didn't have to do this, you know. Not that I'm complaining, use me all you like, but I would have done whatever you asked if you'd been straight with me."

"How did you know?" Kennedy felt her cheeks burn and her pleasure turned to shame. Her languid muscles stiffened, making it uncomfortable to hold his still-stiff cock inside her. She shifted and he slipped from within her, leaving her cold as his thick erection landed on his abdomen with a wet thud. "And why'd you let me tie you up? Why'd you—"

"Kennedy, you're breaking up." Jordan cut in. "Is he secure? Can we come in?"

She dropped her hand so the Shields could hear again as her body began to go numb.

"Don't you think I've heard the rumors of who you work for, Goody Two Shoes?" Knox raised a brow. "Maybe I just wanted to fuck you."

She might have slapped him if she hadn't tried to manipulate him or if he hadn't continued.

"Or maybe I want to cooperate. I admit I didn't believe the rumors about you at first, but there was no way you showing up tonight was a coincidence. You're not the same girl I knew once, now are you? You're harder. Smarter. As sharp as one of your scalpels. But still sweet somewhere deep inside. It was worth it to find out for sure. You didn't have to tie me up. I wouldn't have run from you"

Knox licked his lips, which still glistened with her arousal.

"Shit! What are we waiting for? He knows. Go, go, go!" Marcus shouted as Kennedy heard a rustle from outside followed by the thud of boots on the rickety wooden steps of the cabin.

"You did last time. Fool me once, asshole." She wanted to smack Knox upside his smarmy face, but she refused to cross that line. She hated the things he did to her. How he warped her values and weakened the qualities she respected in herself.

Just like he always had.

What bullshit. She'd barely finished fucking him, had gotten off without even returning the favor, and here she was acting like she was better than him, if only in her own mind.

Rage filled Kennedy, both at herself and at Knox. Together, they were toxic. Now and in the past too. Nothing had changed at all.

Kennedy whimpered and crawled off him backward, grabbing a sheet and wrapping it around her as Sola and Marcus burst into the cabin. Through the open door and windows she could see Nolan, Ransom, Levi, Liam, and Ace blocking every exit.

"At least I finally got a taste of that sweet pussy. Worth it." Knox made a show of licking his glistening and swollen lips, humiliating her in front of her team and making her fists clench in the sheet.

Marcus apparently didn't have the same standards she did, or the same self-restraint. Though his self-control had a legendary reputation, apparently even he had his limits. He strode to the bed and decked Knox, knocking him out cold.

"Damn it, Marcus," Sola snarled as she rushed to Kennedy and wrapped her in a hug before fixing her shirt and skirt to protect what non-existent modesty Kennedy had left.

"He deserved it." In fact, Marcus looked like he might not stop at a single punch.

"Of course he did. I wanted to be the one to do it," Sola huffed as James muttered *Amen* across the comms.

"Is everything secure?" Jordan asked.

"Yeah, boss," Nolan affirmed from his place just outside the door. "We're going to collect our equipment then bring this douche back to the office with us so you can have a chat with him yourself."

The office. The one attached to Kennedy's apartment.

Fuck her life. Because the man she had once loved and now had come around while the guy he'd ruined her for listened and watched was about to be their damn neighbor.

5

Marcus shook his hand out, hoping like hell that Knox's jaw hurt at least as bad as his knuckles did when that bastard woke up. He'd played Kennedy, getting a quickie out of things when he'd known all along what she was up to. Okay, so she hadn't been upfront either, but Marcus only cared about her in this equation.

And if he was jealous as fuck—like the time his best friend in high school had asked Marcus's secret crush to the prom before he'd gotten up the nerve to do it himself, but a million times worse—well, that might have fueled his aggression just a little.

"Get yourselves together. Focus," Jordan snapped. "Liam, Ace, take that shit and load it into our vehicles. We'll get it handed over to the DEA to be disposed of properly."

Their two new recruits sprang into action, lugging the bricks out of the cabin into their waiting fleet. Probably best to do it while Knox was too out of it to object. The guy was a scrapper, his chiseled body dotted with scars and junk tattoos that attested to some hard living. When combined with his ginger hair and skin nearly as light as Kennedy's, dotted with a freckle here and there, it made for an interesting aesthetic. One that Marcus was shocked he didn't find entirely distasteful.

He scrubbed his still-throbbing hands over his face. This assignment was screwing with his head. Or maybe it was the fact that he'd set a personal record for longest gap between lays since Kennedy had taken up residence in his obsessions. He must be hard up if the man who'd just screwed the woman he'd been lusting after for months and who'd wounded her profoundly, enough to scare her away from even the hint of a relationship, was looking fine to him.

Marcus stood guard—over Kennedy or Knox, he couldn't say, maybe both—as Liam and Ace made short work of the drugs. Sola, Ransom, and Levi disassembled the monitoring gear while Aarav manned his sniper post somewhere out in the distance.

If nothing else, they'd kept a crap ton of that hybrid super-drug from hitting the streets. The last batch that had been distributed had been responsible for fifty-seven overdoses in Middletown in a single night. Whether Marcus liked it or not, Knox was valuable. The guy could help save a lot of lives, if he was sincere about his change of heart.

Marcus barely stopped himself from rolling his eyes at that. Especially when the dude groaned and wrestled his eyes open. Kennedy, her clothes mostly in order again even if the pretty rosy flush on her cheeks was still blatant, scooted between Knox and Marcus.

"Thanks." Knox flashed her a lopsided grin. "Your bodyguard here has a heck of a right hook."

"I should let him hit you again." Kennedy crossed her arms and glared at Knox.

"Oh, come on. It's pretty obvious we still have plenty of chemistry," Knox murmured.

"You know what else has chemistry?" Kennedy asked as she bent over and took care of disposing his condom, yanking his jeans up, and tucking his half-hard cock back into his pants before zipping them without nearly enough caution. When the guy didn't screech, Marcus figured she hadn't snagged his cock. "Drugs. But those aren't good for you either. I've kicked the habit I formed for you, Knox."

The bastard smirked while Kennedy handled his dick, even if it was with the detached, professional demeanor she used when she examined patients in the field. "Didn't seem like it when you were wringing that thing dry."

"Do I have to knock your ass out again?" Marcus growled as he hovered over Kennedy's shoulder protectively. Kennedy jerked as if she'd forgotten he was there. Did she and Knox always have this tunnel vision thing going on when they were together or was she intentionally trying to block Marcus out because she was ashamed he'd heard her getting off with her ex?

Marcus was going to have to have a discussion to unpack that with her later. He didn't want any emotional bullshit getting between them and making things awkward. Not in their personal life and definitely not on the job, when their lives so often depended on each other's clear thinking.

He was certain now that this admittedly hot asswipe tied to the bed in front of him was the man who'd screwed him out of the amazing relationship he knew he could have had with Kennedy if she hadn't been too gun-shy to let him in.

Marcus was honest enough with himself to admit that frustration had been a big part of why he'd let the guy have a taste of his fist a minute ago. Because after the single kiss he'd shared with Kennedy not too long ago, he had no doubts about how incredible it would be if they were partners both on and off the job, and now he was even more certain than ever that she would never let him in.

Knox still had a death grip on her heart. Motherfucker.

"You know what? You're not any better than him. Hovering. Acting like a cave man. You don't have any claim on me." Kennedy didn't really need to remind Marcus of the obvious.

"I was trying to protect you." He held his hands up, palms out, and retreated the small step across the rough plank floor that the confined space permitted. "You've made it abundantly clear you're not into me like that."

Kennedy winced. "This isn't the time or place…"

"You're right. I'm sorry." Marcus forced his jaw to relax, then said, "Later."

She nodded once, curtly.

Knox was staring between them, reclining with his ankles crossed and his head pillowed on his folded wrists as if he'd chosen to languish there, tied up before them. Marcus should be careful not to give away too much, though it was probably obvious to everyone—their boss included—by now that he had a pretty constant hard-on for their team's medic.

Great.

"So where exactly are you taking me?" Knox wondered.

"You don't need to know the details." Marcus angled

himself away, then spoke to their coordinator. "James, are you ready for us to load him in with the rest of the cargo?"

"Slight change of plans, folks. I hate to break up this lovely reunion, but you're about to have company..." James's warning had them all standing straight and whipping their stares toward the door and the tiny gravel road that wound through the woods to the cabin. If someone approached, they would be boxed in. "Three black SUVs are speeding in from the west. You have less than a minute."

"Son of a bitch!" Ace snarled before bolting to the vehicles and the additional stash of weapons and ammunition they kept in them.

Though Knox couldn't hear James's warning, the Shields' collective call to attention must have told him what was happening clearly enough.

"Fuck, fuck, fuck." Knox struggled against the restraints holding his hands over his head. He stared up at Kennedy, who still refused to meet his gaze, her face flushed and her eyes bright despite her anger. "Let me loose or I'll be a sitting duck."

"Aren't they your friends? What makes you think they're coming for you and not us for fucking with you and stealing their shit?" Marcus asked Knox.

"We both know why." Knox's cheeks turned maroon as he wrenched his arms, unsuccessful in wriggling from the leather strap holding him tight. Kennedy had done a hell of a job lashing him to the headboard. "Because I'm not on their team anymore."

"Well, you're sure as hell not on ours." Marcus drew two guns from their holsters and flicked the safeties off. "Sit tight and we'll load you up to take you to our safe house after we exterminate these snakes."

6

———

Knox rattled the whole damn piece-of-shit headboard as he tried to get loose. At least the news of the impending raid had helped deflate the rest of his hard-on. He couldn't believe he'd finally been inside the woman of his fantasies. Even if he hadn't come, he'd sure as hell enjoyed making sure she did.

"Kennedy, come on." He tried appealing to her rational side. "This is stupid. Let me loose so I can help. You don't even have a weapon, do you?"

She shook her head and refused to meet his gaze as she peeked out the window. "Didn't want to blow my cover. Not that it mattered."

"Come away from there at least." Knox winced. "I hope your friends are as good as the rumblings I've heard about them."

As if on cue, the skid of tires on gravel was punctuated by the shattering of auto glass. Knox hadn't heard any gunshots, which could only mean one thing. "You have snipers?"

She hesitated, as if unwilling to confirm even the most basic info. He didn't blame her for not trusting him, but it still stung considering they were officially in the midst of a life-or-death situation.

"I'm not an idiot, you know. And I've spent my whole life around this bullshit." Knox wasn't proud of it, but he at least did her the courtesy of being honest. Especially about things she already knew in her gut even if they hadn't stayed pen pals for him to fill her in on the details of his daily activities.

"Just one." She crouched beside the bed, where she'd be as obscured as possible if anyone entered. It wasn't much but it was something. "One really good one, though. He can't get them all because of the trees. It's going to get ugly. I hope Sola has my kit close."

"Is that the brunette?"

Kennedy nodded.

Her calm statement of the facts both freaked him out and sort of turned him on. This shouldn't be normal. Not even for a street rat like him. Certainly not for a highly educated doctor like her. But the fact that she could handle the pressure, and work to undo the terrible things that came from situations like this, only increased his admiration for her.

It was about then that the shots began to ring out along with shouts that Knox recognized as commands from the Vipers. The Shields were dead silent as they picked off his former associates. He didn't bother to lie to himself and call them friends since they were a snarled mess of users, power-hungry psychos, and derelicts, who stuck together because there wasn't a better option.

Kennedy tipped her head, her eyes half-shut as she listened to her team on the comm he hadn't been able to make out, even though he figured she was wearing one. "Almost clear. Three left. Marcus is engaging one in hand-to-hand."

Her knuckles turned white as she clutched her abdomen. The tension he'd felt between those two had nothing to do with work shit. There was something there, something that made Knox envious despite having sacrificed any claim he had on Kennedy years ago and having been fused with her so recently. "You like that asshole? I always said you had terrible taste in men."

Kennedy glared at him.

Knox wasn't smart enough to keep his big mouth shut. "I mean, he's fine and all, built too, but don't you think it's a bad idea to fuck your coworkers, especially in a job like this?"

"Yes. That's exactly why we don't do that." She looked away, but not before he saw the profound sadness in her beautiful blue eyes. He wondered if it was more than only that keeping them apart, but he didn't expect for her to revert to best friend status with him, given how he'd fucked over their bond.

Before Knox could make things even worse, she bolted to her feet.

"What?" Knox tried to follow until his hands yanked him back.

There wasn't time for her to answer before a lone Viper smashed through the door and into their hidey-hole. *Son of a bitch!*

"Convenient." Larry paused long enough for a slow grin to spread across his scarred face. "I'll thank your lady here for making it easy for me to get rid of our little problem. Did you really think you were going to get away with turning on us, you asshole?"

It happened so fast, Knox couldn't think. He could only react. Larry raised his gun and aimed it at Knox. Kennedy unleashed an inhuman scream and slammed into the guy from the side. Her slender weight didn't do as much as she might have hoped and she bounced off. She clearly had some training as she swiped at his knees and then his weapon arm, but no one was a match in those close quarters for someone with a gun. Especially when they had no weapon of their own.

Knox arched then yanked, a feral roar accompanying his lurch. The leather stayed knotted around his wrists, but the shitty headboard didn't stand a chance against his combined terror and rage. He ripped the post loose from the frame and freed himself, carrying his momentum forward.

He barreled into the bastard somewhere around knee level, knocking him to the ground. Knox swung his bound wrists, bashing Larry across the face, before smothering him as best he could. He used his elbows, knees, and even his teeth to inflict as much pain and distraction on the guy as he could. It wasn't enough though, or maybe when Knox's knee connected somewhere in the region of Larry's balls, his hand jerked reflexively.

Because his gun went off.

Knox bellowed, "No!"

He frantically tried to see if Kennedy was okay, but the world was a flurry of chaos and confusion.

At the same time, Marcus appeared in the doorway, took aim, and blew Larry's fucking head off with no regard to Knox's safety given his proximity to the bastard.

Covered in blood and gore, his ears ringing so loud he didn't know if he'd ever hear again, Knox rolled to the side.

"Knox!" Kennedy was there, kicking aside the corpse to get to him.

To Knox's surprise, Marcus helped her uncover him even as he barked into his comm, "Got the last one. Fuck. That was close."

Knox went limp. It had been *far too fucking close*. He'd thought he'd hit rock bottom before, but now he realized that if he'd caused Kennedy harm, he would have been worse than dead.

"Oh God. Marcus. Someone bring me my kit. Now! Knox is hit. Who else is hurt and how bad? Give me a rundown so I can prioritize." Kennedy went into some sort of medic mode that Knox had never witnessed before. She was calm, efficient, and oh so capable. She was so glorious it took him a minute to register what she'd said.

Him? He stared down at his torso, and sure enough, there was a long streak of black and blood stretching from his ribs to his nipple on the opposite side. Oh, fuck. And there went the pain to go with it. Huh.

"It's just a graze. I'm fine." But damn, did it burn. "See if anyone else needs you first."

Kennedy bit her lip as she scanned him from head to toe, then gave a curt nod. But before she turned away entirely he lifted his bound hands and snagged one of hers. "Don't ever scare me like that again."

"I'm not the one that tried to stop a bullet with my fucking body." She glared at him, which was enough to reassure him she was perfectly fine.

He chuckled. "Don't lie, baby. I saw you charge that guy. You would have done the same for me. I love you too."

He'd meant it as a joke, but they both knew it wasn't. He'd always adored her and she him. Could there be even a tiny sliver of that devotion left alive after all the time and damage he'd done to them both?

Kennedy jerked as if another round had gone off mere feet from them. Kind of telling since she didn't so much as flinch when surrounded by a dead man and parts that used to be inside his skull strewn about.

She shook her head, then snapped, "Ace is hurt worse. He needs me. I'll be back as soon as I can."

With that, she dashed out the door and into the yard, dotted with unmoving bodies, dressed in black. Her teammates were already picking up the garbage, loading bodies into the back of a pickup truck and covering them with a tarp for disposal who knew where.

Knox swiped gore from his face. He levered himself first to his knees and then to his feet. If he swayed a little, he was glad Marcus didn't mention it. The other man stood frozen, his boots planted as he stared at the spot Kennedy had been standing. "She really did what you said? She charged that guy with no weapon?"

"Yup." Knox shook his head, knowing he'd never get the image out of his mind as long as he lived. "Took ten years off my life."

Marcus swung his gaze to Knox then, and the impact of it nearly sent him sprawling on his ass again. He sank onto the edge of the bed, unwilling to embarrass himself in front of the man who obviously deserved Kennedy even if Knox had fucked her up too much to see it for herself.

"I owe you." Marcus came forward then and knelt, surprising the fuck out of Knox when he began to pick at the knot on the leather cord. He unwound it gently and looked up, his eyes a curious mixture of brown and gold that fascinated Knox. "I couldn't stop that asshole. I tried.

He slipped by as I was taking care of his buddy. She could have died if it wasn't for you."

"She wouldn't have even been here if it wasn't for me." Knox was no hero. No one knew it better than him. He certainly hadn't earned the profound gratitude radiating from Marcus.

"If something had happened to her, I never would have survived it," Marcus murmured, his hand on his comm, probably muting it. "So you saved me too today. I won't forget this."

"I, uh..." Knox swallowed, moved by the kindness and grace of a near stranger.

But the moment was fleeting. The brunette who'd shot daggers at him earlier, Sola he thought Kennedy had called her, joined them in the cabin. She wasn't nearly as quick to forgive how he'd taken advantage of the situation, and Kennedy, earlier. It made him feel oddly comforted to know Kennedy had so many tight friends. "Looks like I'm your ride, asshole. It was obvious from your friend here that they'd made you, so we're your only option. Jordan says you can have a place with us so long as you're willing to cooperate."

Marcus looked to Knox then, his face slack but his eyes urging Knox not to make the wrong decision. For once in his life, he wanted to do the right thing. He wanted to belong among people like this, who fought for goodness and light, even if they had to do some very dark things.

"Like you said, it's not like I have a choice." Knox shrugged, the motion making it feel like he ripped his chest in half. He sucked in a ragged breath.

Then Kennedy was back, her platinum-blond hair streaming behind her if now with a few crimson streaks.

Her bubblegum-pink tank top and short skirt, both splashed with blood, making them seem tie-dyed, clashed with the neat, professional black case she carried as she marched to the bed. She flipped it open and withdrew sterile sealed instruments and a shit-ton of bandages before putting on a fresh pair of gloves.

"Lie back," she commanded.

"I'd like to finish what we started too." Knox couldn't help his protective instincts, which insisted he make light of the situation when the air was so heavy he could hardly breathe.

Marcus shook his head and Sola looked like she might make good on her promise to deck him next. But the corner of Kennedy's lips quirked up and he figured she still appreciated his sick sense of humor like she always had. She'd been the only woman who ever got him.

Only with Riggs had he found a companionship that came close. And look how that had ended. He'd gotten the guy killed.

Knox did flop onto the bed then, exhausted. Pain began to radiate from his wound despite the care Kennedy took to be gentle as she wiped away the blood oozing from it.

"I think you could use a few stiches here, and here." She pressed the edges of the graze together in a couple of spots, as if picturing how best to close it. "Just to keep your chest looking pretty."

"You like it, huh?" Knox distracted himself by teasing her, while making her friends glower.

Kennedy ignored him for the most part and focused on her craft. Confidence was sexy. And in this she didn't hesitate. She cleaned his injury, sewed him up, and bandaged him before he could really register all that had happened that evening.

His life had taken a major turn, and for once, he desperately wanted to not fuck it up.

Knox must have lost more blood than he'd realized, or maybe pure exhaustion caught up with him after the death of his lover, quitting drugs and alcohol cold turkey, and being turned on by the organization he'd been a part of for a decade. When Kennedy finished, he struggled to sit up again.

To his surprise, Marcus reached out, banding one of his impressive arms around Knox and levering him to his feet. He kept it there as he ushered Knox to a waiting vehicle.

Sola slid into the driver's side and a man with dark, wavy hair took the passenger seat beside her. When he spoke, it was with an accent that sounded Indian to Knox. "Liam says Ace is stable. Thanks to you, Kennedy."

"Let's go. I'll need to take him into the clinic for X-rays. I'm worried the bullet might have shattered the bone, and if so, I'll need to find an orthopedic specialist who doesn't ask too many questions to put a few plates and screws in there for us. If not, I can set it myself at headquarters. Either way, it's going to be a shitty ride home for him."

Marcus boosted Knox into the second row of the SUV, then walked Kennedy around to the opposite side. She slid into the middle, and Marcus book ended her. He squeezed her hand for a little longer than was simply polite or reassuring for a teammate.

Knox tried to do the same to her hand on his side, but she withdrew and leaned closer to Marcus instead.

"Kennedy, I'm sorry," Knox said.

"For fucking me even though you knew it was a setup?

Why? I did the same to you. Or for abandoning me to do drugs and the bullshit that got you here in the first place? It's yourself you have to apologize to for that." Her head dropped forward and she pinched the bridge of her nose. "Things could have been so different."

"Nah, they couldn't." Knox refused to believe he'd fucked up that badly or it would rip him the rest of the way open like the bullet he'd been willing to take for her hadn't managed to do. "I'm fucked up. It would have ruined us eventually. No matter what. I only regret that I got you involved. I am sorry, and I'll do my best to make it right now."

Sola exchanged a glance with the guy sitting beside her, and Knox noticed she didn't bust his balls anymore despite having left himself vulnerable to any number of jabs that he rightfully deserved.

"How about you be quiet for the rest of the trip?" Kennedy said softly as the adrenaline that had kept her going obviously began to leach from her bloodstream. She closed her eyes and leaned to her right, resting against Marcus, who curled his arm around her shoulder and glared at Knox.

Without raising her head, she murmured, "After today, everyone knows exactly how messed up I am too. So please, can we let it go? Work on yourself and let me do the same so I can stop hurting the people I actually care about."

Ouch. He'd rather have been shot again than hear the obvious truth fall from her lips.

Even in the depths of his misery, he didn't miss the apologetic look Sola sent her navigator. Was there more going on between them? Were each of them a little—or a lot—screwed up?

"After today, I get it," Marcus whispered to her, though in the quiet of the car, everyone could hear his kindness shining through. "I'm sorry I didn't understand before. I won't pressure you for something you're not able to give."

Kennedy nodded against his shoulder and closed her eyes, whether dozing off or blocking out the rest of the world so she could focus on Ace when they arrived. No one bothered her again for the rest of the journey.

It was the look Marcus shot Knox, full of compassion and understanding, that stuck in his mind. Despite their differences, they had an awful lot in common, including caring deeply for a woman they didn't stand a chance with.

7

Kennedy crossed her legs as she sat at the glossy table in the command room of the Shields' headquarters. She wished she'd taken five minutes to run up to her apartment and change out of the ridiculous outfit Sola had lent her, or at least to put on new underwear. The air conditioning made her very aware of every breeze passing through the room.

Better not to think about how she'd lost them.

"Good job today, team." Jordan was wrapping up his debriefing. They'd already contacted an agent for Ransom and Levi to meet up with and transfer the stash they'd confiscated. Liam was at the hospital relaying updates on Ace's condition after persuading the staff there that his injuries were due to an accidental discharge of his firearm. Knox was hanging out in one of their "waiting rooms" which, though cozy, had no windows and were essentially fancy cells. Meanwhile, Kennedy was trying to ignore the hot mess she'd made of her life by fucking the ex she'd never gotten over while the man she wished she could have a future with watched and listened.

She squirmed in her chair, wondering why that thought made her wish she could do it again. Lying to herself, or to any of the other Shields, would be pointless. They'd all borne witness to exactly how much she'd enjoyed herself.

Shit.

"Last two items..." Jordan looked to her then. "Kennedy, take blood samples from Knox and run a full battery of tests on him. Both for his own health and safety, and for your peace of mind as well."

"Oh." She blinked—of course she should have thought of that herself. And likely would have if she wasn't trying so hard to smother her residual emotions from their exchange. The ramifications of their quickie might ripple through her life for a long time to come. "Sure. Will do."

"Get him set up with counseling and an addiction specialist to help him stay sober. Maybe Gavyn or Roman can suggest a sponsor who could be discreet if they're not interested personally." He referred to their friends, who'd met at rehab. Gavyn owned the Hot Rides motorcycle shop and Roman was a mechanic at its classic car sister garage, Hot Rods. Jordan cleared his throat and added, "I think it would be best if you took some time on the clock to do the same. In fact, I'm going to require you attend five sessions. If you want to keep going beyond those, that's fine too."

"Me?" She choked on a reflexive denial. Maybe it wasn't a horrible idea.

"He's right, Kennedy. You should do it." Sola nudged her. As an operative skilled in seduction, she would understand the impact making herself so vulnerable could have. The difference being Sola had never slept with someone she cared about for the job.

"Okay, I will. Thanks."

Jordan nodded, then turned to Marcus. "We're going to need to house our guest upstairs somewhere. I realize we have plenty of empty apartments, but—"

"Oh boy." Aarav whistled low, as if he'd already guessed what was coming next.

"—given the fact that Knox has played for both sides, and is in a pretty bleak situation, we don't want to take any chances on him contacting a Viper or maybe harming himself."

Kennedy blinked. Why did that thought bring out the goose bumps on her bare legs when even the arctic AC hadn't? She didn't want to give a shit about Knox. Too late.

"Fuck no." Marcus stiffened. "You want me to babysit him?"

"I'd make the newbies do it, but..." Jordan shrugged. Ace wasn't going to be in any physical condition to be fending off a man as streetwise and tough as Knox any time soon, and Liam was going to be preoccupied with Ace. If Kennedy wasn't mistaken, she thought they might be more than simply field partners at the Shields.

"Ransom and Levi?" Marcus never argued with Jordan or turned down an assignment. It raised more than a few brows around the table.

"They already have the exchange set up with the DEA agent, who is familiar with Ransom. We can't switch our operative now." Jordan crossed his arms.

"What about Nolan?" Marcus looked around the room. "Aarav? Sola and Ruby? *Anyone* else? Come on, somebody, help me out here."

"I have a feeling you'll be properly motivated to keep

an extra close watch on our guest." Jordan smirked while the others chuckled. Kennedy didn't join in. She noticed Marcus hadn't mentioned her in his laundry list. Was it because he knew her judgment couldn't be trusted when Knox was around?

Or was he jealous of them and what they might get up to if left alone?

She shot him a side-eyed glance, but he refused to meet her stare. Great.

"Yeah, fine." Marcus grumbled. "But don't blame me if he ends up with another black eye. He's got a smart mouth and I'm not in the mood for it."

Kennedy couldn't argue with that. It also happened to be a mouth capable of imparting a thousand times more potent pleasure than her favorite toy. And now she knew it for sure instead of only suspecting that to be the case, she was never going to stop reliving the moment he'd gone down on her in her fantasies. Damn him.

"It'd be a much better tactic to befriend him, or at least make it seem like you have." Jordan shrugged one shoulder.

"Now you're asking for too much." Marcus sliced a hand through the air.

"All right, that's it. Everyone get some rest and make sure you're staying alert both when you're on duty and when you're away from headquarters, especially around our friends at Hot Rods, Hot Rides, the Powertools construction sites, and other innocent bystanders. The Vipers aren't going to slither away once they figure out who has their guy. This isn't over." Jordan stood and everyone else followed suit, milling around to discuss plans for dinner or workouts before crashing.

For the first time ever, Kennedy felt out of place in

their midst. Probably because she respected the hell out of them but right then she wasn't sure she could say the same of herself.

Sola and Ruby edged closer. Sola lowered her voice and asked, "You okay?"

"Yeah, I guess. Got a few orgasms out of the deal—what's to complain about?" Kennedy tried to shrug it off.

"Uh oh." Ruby winced, then tossed her flaming red hair over her shoulder. "You're a terrible liar. Good thing you stick to medic duties most of the time."

"I have chocolate and a whole playlist of kickboxing videos queued up if you want to vent or let off some steam upstairs," Sola suggested, flinging a glance at Aarav.

Kennedy wondered what he'd done or if existing and tempting Sola without acting on whatever latent desire pulsed between them was enough to have her beating the shit out of her punching bag every evening. Aarav glanced in their direction as if he could sense Sola's stare. Rather than engage in their discussion, he ducked out of the room.

"Thanks, but nah. I just need some time to decompress and forget that ever happened." Kennedy's fist clenched even as she said it.

Sola's eyes narrowed. "Hold on. Are you sure you're not pissed because you thought he was into you and then you found out he'd already made you?"

Kennedy pinched the bridge of her nose in an attempt to keep her eyes from tearing up. "Is it that obvious? I thought he fucking wanted me."

"Girl, I saw the size of that boner while I was manning the video feeds. He definitely did." Ruby snorted. "Hell, I saved some still shots and clips for evidence and would be happy to email them to you if you want to verify for yourself."

"Don't get your ass fired." Sola laughed. "I like having you around, balancing out all this testosterone."

"Knox probably got off on outsmarting me." Kennedy tried not to pout. "He had no trouble leaving me behind before. I don't mean anything to him. Never did."

"He obviously means a lot to you." Sola grimaced. "That would piss me off too. Don't let it get you down. If he's a manipulative asshole, he doesn't deserve you. And if he didn't see that any man would be lucky to have you—especially him—and let you go, then he's an idiot. Either way, you don't need trash like that in your life."

"Thanks." Kennedy couldn't help but smile a bit at the fierce protectiveness of her friends. Maybe they didn't think as badly of her as she did of herself at that moment.

James slipped into their circle. "Not that I was eavesdropping—okay, I totally was—but yes to everything Sola said. Especially when you have a damn good Door Number Two standing right over there."

Their operations manager, who was a reformed construction worker with a superhero's sidekick complex, jerked his chin very blatantly in Marcus's direction. As much as Kennedy wanted to be annoyed with him and his matchmaker ways, it would be impossible to be irritated with James. She could understand why his husband and their wife were obsessed with their adorkable lover.

"I've done enough of opening things up today." Kennedy groaned. "In fact, as soon as I finish Knox's blood work, I think I'll hit the hot tub."

"Sore, huh?" James winked. "Gotta love that."

He would know since he enjoyed the attention of not only his two spouses but the rest of their polyamorous friends on the Powertools crew. From what she'd heard, sometimes all in one evening too. She had no idea how he managed that when one man for a few minutes had made her see stars.

"I'm not an expert like you," she teased, glad things weren't as awkward as she'd expected.

He preened. "Speaking of that, I have to get home. The Powertools are waiting for me to celebrate Dave's birthday. Nolan, you ready?"

The other guy flashed a wide grin as he slung an arm around James's shoulders. "Yeah. But you don't need me to give you a ride anymore."

"Of course I do. Since you backed over my baby..." James froze. "Wait! Is my car fixed?" His micro hybrid sedan had taken a few beatings lately, most recently when Nolan had smooshed it at the opening of the headquarters. Good thing they had a hell of a lot of mechanic friends.

"Waiting outside for you. I even had Sally put on some extra protectant over her paint job to keep it looking spiffy for you." Nolan twitched his shoulder toward the door. "Let's go check it out."

"I'm going to go do that. You're going to stay far, far away from him." James wagged a finger at Nolan as they headed for the parking lot. But before he left the room he jogged back and hugged Kennedy, whispering in her ear, "You'll figure this out. Just remember we love you and no one thinks less of you for doing your job today, even if your feelings got tangled up in that mess."

She sighed. "Thanks."

And then he was gone, busting Nolan's balls the whole way out of hearing.

Ransom and Levi headed out to get ready for their

drop off, and Aarav approached to ask Sola if she wanted to order with him from the Thai restaurant they both loved despite the consequences the twelve-chilis-out-of-ten spice level must wreak on their intestines.

Ruby shot her a look every woman knew. One that asked if she was okay being left alone with Marcus...and Knox. God help her.

Kennedy waved and Ruby nodded. "Text me if you change your mind and want some company later."

"Will do. Thanks." Kennedy genuinely appreciated the offer and how easy they were making this on her. She should have given the Shields more credit. They weren't judgmental assholes, and they accepted her, flaws and all.

When they were alone, the silence stretched between her and Marcus. She had no idea what to say to him. So she was glad when he broke the tension. "If you're not comfortable being so close to him, I'll have Jordan call in a nurse."

"Thanks, but I think we both know I don't have any aversion to touching him." Kennedy ducked her head, but he was having none of that.

Marcus put one of his thick fingers beneath her chin and lifted it so that they were staring into each other's eyes from inches apart. "Tell me something. He's the guy, isn't he? The asshole who hurt you. The one who made you afraid to try again."

"He's the person who showed me what bad decisions I make when I let my heart, or my hormones, override my brain." She didn't bother to deny it. "And for good reason. Look what happened after I got a taste of him again. I forgot every single lesson he taught me before. I have no self-control—"

"Bullshit." Marcus wasn't having any of that. "I mean,

we kissed and you had no trouble telling me to back off. You're plenty capable of shutting down your desires. You didn't want to. And neither did he. I saw what happened in the cabin earlier. That wasn't all for show."

Kennedy drew in a shaky breath, wishing she had the right to crash into Marcus's broad chest and ask him to hold her until she found solid footing again. He reached out and steadied her with one hand on her shoulder.

"Nothing you did today was wrong and it doesn't change one damn thing about how I think of you, okay?" Marcus's eyes weren't accusing; they were kind. Which made it impossible to reject the embrace he offered with outstretched arms. She went into them and he held her close, stroking her hair as he murmured, "If I'm being honest, it was the hottest thing I've ever seen. You were every bit as passionate as I've imagined. I've never been so jealous in my entire life."

"Yeah?" It was a moment of weakness, but right then she needed reassurance.

So when he leaned in and fit his lips to hers, she didn't resist his kiss.

The gentle swaddle of his arms had nothing in common with the possession of his mouth. This time he didn't stop at a butterfly brush of it across hers as he had the night of the grand opening party. No, right then he showed her what it could be like if she ever gave in and let him do all the things his heated stares promised he'd like to with her.

Kennedy must have been a fool to deny them both this, and more, for so long. With Marcus, there was no wondering, no games. He had always been honest with her, and if he said he would be there, for a night or longer, she could believe him.

She leaned into him, counting on him to keep them steady as their kiss went on and on until she had to breathe or pass out. Then she stepped back and gulped air as she stared at his dilated eyes and the pulse pounding in his neck.

Kennedy suppressed every urge she had to cling to Marcus and instead widened the chasm between them with another pace toward the waiting room and the job she still had left to do.

"I'll be right here if you need anything." Marcus cracked his knuckles. "I dare him to give me a reason."

"If you break his nose, I'll just have more work setting it."

"Plus you don't want me to mess up his pretty fucking face." Marcus grunted.

Kennedy's stride hitched at that. Had she really seen a flash of appreciation in his gaze? "You think Knox is handsome?"

"Hot as fuck. Yeah, I see why you're hung up on him. Sexy, smart talker, badass, and lost. Not to mention that big fucking dick he obviously knows how to use. It's an irresistible combination, isn't it?" Marcus shrugged as if it was no big deal.

Okay. Well. She'd had no idea he was that open-minded. She wracked her brain but definitely would have remembered if he'd ever mentioned being bisexual. Then again, she'd purposefully steered their late-night conversations from steamy territory lest she be enticed to break her vow of celibacy.

"I guess so." She licked the lingering taste of him from her bottom lip as she looked at him in a whole new light.

"Go. I'll be waiting to take him upstairs when you're done."

Kennedy nodded, then spun on her heel, only fully realizing at that moment that she'd now have not only one but two extraordinary temptations living right across the hall.

Damn it. She was going to need to order some more batteries.

8

Marcus trudged from his bedroom when the aroma of coffee and something cinnamon-y penetrated his dreams. Dreams where instead of prowling the woods while Sola rolled her eyes at his obvious possessive jealousy, he had caved to the urge to bust in on Kennedy and Knox in that rickety cabin and done his best to make her come apart for him like she had for her bastard of an ex.

He'd woken up with an erection at least as solid as the one he'd had while on their op the day before and without the privacy to do anything about it. So Marcus had splayed on his bed, ruminating about the even shittier moments of the day before—like the one where he'd thought that stray Viper was going to murder Kennedy before he could do anything to stop it.

Or how he had been forced to protect the man who'd fucked his obsession. Worse, Knox had made sure—even in those unusual circumstances—that she'd enjoyed it and then had the audacity to get credit for saving her life

69

even though he'd been the one to put her in harm's way in the first place.

Marcus was completely screwed up about the whole operation.

Everything regarding the situation made him uncomfortable. Physically, as he shifted his deflated package and aching balls, and mentally also.

Marcus glared at Knox as he entered the kitchen. The other man had made himself right at home in Marcus's damn apartment, which was still pretty new even to him. He loved living so close to Kennedy and the rest of the team, since it was impossible for outsiders to understand what his job entailed unless they'd also been some sort of soldier or undercover agent. Especially since so much of what he did wasn't something he could discuss in polite company.

And now that newfound sense of sanctuary had been shattered by Knox, who became the focal point for his bad mood.

"Hope you don't mind. I was starving." Knox gestured to the bowl of oatmeal with cinnamon on top neatly positioned on the placemat in front of him with the banana he was peeling as he spoke. "I made enough for both of us, plus a pot of coffee. And I got the ingredients together for some fresh fruit smoothies, but I was waiting for you to wake up to turn on the blender."

Marcus took one look at Knox, shirtless, at his dining room table, popping a big chunk of the now-peeled banana into his mouth and spun away with a grunt. Son of a bitch, was he going to deep throat the thing or eat it?

"Not a morning person, huh?" Knox asked, incredibly bubbly for someone on the run from a gang of some of the baddest motherfuckers on the planet. Then again, he had escaped near certain death the day before with bonus sex thrown in to make his evasion even sweeter.

Sure, he hadn't come but still, it would have been an honor to pleasure Kennedy.

Marcus poured himself a mug of coffee and plopped into the seat farthest away from Knox. That left them at opposite ends of the table, staring each other down. It irritated him more that he didn't hate the scenery.

"Maybe I could borrow a T-shirt and some shorts?" Knox winced as he looked down at his bare torso. The graze from the day before had morphed into a rainbow of bruises and raw skin from yellow to red to purple. Marcus didn't check under the table, but he was pretty sure Knox was perched on his brand-new chair in his briefs since he didn't have any other options except the jeans he'd been wearing the day before. His shirt had been ruined when he'd nearly traded his life for Kennedy's.

Marcus shifted guiltily as he remembered how much he owed this prick.

"Yeah, of course." He started to stand.

"Eat first." Knox was surprisingly considerate. "Here, let me warm your oatmeal and get those smoothies blended. I assume you work out a lot. You're going to need a solid breakfast before you hit the gym."

Marcus opened his mouth to object but, well, Knox wasn't wrong. "Uh. I guess. Thanks."

His new and very temporary roommate made it damn hard to hate him. With his back turned, Marcus allowed himself to stare at the expanse of light, almost pink skin dotted with freckles on his shoulder blades. It complemented his ginger hair and made a perfect canvas for the Viper tattoo snaking its way up his spine. It was a shame it wasn't better quality work, although Marcus despised what it represented.

Figured, Kennedy had an eye for hot men. But both of them would do well to remember that this was the person who'd betrayed her once and would likely do so again given half a chance.

That didn't stop Marcus's assessing gaze from sliding lower to Knox's tight ass, which filled out his black briefs perfectly, then on to his thighs and calves. While they weren't bulked, they were cut and without a single bit of fat to mar the shape of his muscles.

"You're no stranger to exercise, yourself." Marcus hadn't meant to say that. Damn it. He needed to get more of this coffee into his system before he did something stupid, like pinning the man up against the counter so they could relieve some of the sexual tension neither of them had gotten to blow off yesterday.

Knox glanced over his shoulder with a wicked grin that promised he knew Marcus had been staring. Then he turned on the blender so neither of them had to respond. When he finished, he poured them each some and delivered Marcus's before washing out the glass pitcher and placing it upside down in the drying rack. He wiped the counter, the appliance, and wrung out the dishrag before carrying his own serving back to the table.

Marcus took several gulps to cool himself off from the inside out. And damn if it wasn't good. He held the glass up and stared at it as if he could see the individual ingredients. "What'd you put in this?"

"Mango, pineapple, lime, yogurt, and protein powder." Knox hummed as he drained his glass too. "It's been a long time since I've had fresh fruit."

"The Viper den kitchen isn't stocked?" Marcus regretted asking the instant the question left his lips.

Knox glanced away at that. "Maybe. But for a long time, food wasn't what I was craving. It's been a few months now that I've been clean and, well, I'm still working on regaining muscle and building my stamina. I abused myself plenty over the past ten years and it had gotten really bad. All my bones were poking out and... well, it wasn't pretty."

He set his drink down as if his appetite had vanished just thinking about it. And somehow that made Marcus feel like shit when he shouldn't care. The guy had done that to himself, hadn't he?

He was sick. Marcus could hear Kennedy scolding him even if she wasn't there.

So he figured he owed it to Knox to offer him an olive branch. If nothing else, for saving Kennedy. "Well, we have a hell of a gym downstairs. You're welcome to work out with me whenever."

"Yeah?" Knox asked, perking up.

"Of course." Marcus tried not to think about how much more annoying it would be to spend time with the guy when his muscles were straining, he was glistening with sweat, and they were boosting their serotonin together. He'd have to concentrate to make sure he didn't drop a dumbbell on something important while ogling Knox.

It had been a long time since a guy caught his interest, and it didn't happen very often. Of course it would be this one. He must like to torture himself with things he couldn't have. First, Kennedy and now Knox. Both completely emotionally unavailable. Now with additional landmines of their past relationships to make it even more treacherous.

"Did Kennedy clear you for activity?" Marcus wondered, studying Knox's chest.

"What she doesn't know won't hurt her."

"But it might injure you. Besides, we don't operate that way around here." Marcus couldn't stand half-truths or mind games. "I won't lie for you. So if she asks, it's your balls on the line."

Knox nodded and sipped his smoothie again. "Fair enough. But if I don't do something to burn off my nerves or...uh, you know. Like cravings and stuff... Sometimes exercise is all that works to distract myself."

"Oh." Marcus stared at his smoothie, trying not to make Knox any more uncomfortable. "Then yeah. Let's give ourselves a half hour to digest and find you some clothes. I prefer to lift before cardio. Sound good?"

"It does, but don't laugh when I can't keep up." Knox winced.

Damn it. Why did Marcus feel the need to soothe the guy's insecurities? Was it because he knew Kennedy loved the dumb fuck? Or because it was his job to keep the guy stable enough to be a useful asset to the Shields? Or maybe because there was some sort of charismatic quality to the dude.

Ugh. He suddenly understood why Kennedy hadn't been able to get over Knox even though he hadn't found himself attracted to many men in the past. Sure, he appreciated a fine body, and hanging around with the polyamorous friends he'd made in the Powertools, Hot Rods, and Hot Rides gangs had opened his eyes—and his mind—to the infinite combinations someone could find love in, but he never really expected that for himself.

Hell, he'd never dared to hope he'd find more than a hookup, to be honest. But first Kennedy and now Knox were giving him ideas he'd be better off forgetting.

"I'm not the kind of guy who'd make fun of anyone committed to improving themselves." Marcus crossed his arms to keep his hands firmly by his sides. "I get that what you're going through is tough and I respect you for sticking it out."

"The drug thing or the Viper thing?" Knox glanced up.

"Both. And especially the not-hurting-Kennedy-again thing."

Knox nodded. "Roger that. I never meant to, you know? Me leaving had nothing to do with her."

Marcus held his hands up. "That sounds like something you should talk to her about, not me."

A couple hours later they'd finished a circuit on the weight machines and were in a steady jog side-by-side on the treadmills when Knox coughed. He stumbled but kept going, though one hand clutched his chest and his fair skin told the truth he was apparently unwilling to voice. Flushed and bright, sweat pouring from his face, and his breathing labored, he'd had enough.

Marcus looked over and called it. "That's good enough for me. You done?" Of course, on an ordinary day he'd have the pace set to twice what they'd been doing and could have gone for another thirty minutes while singing along to the radio.

"Thanks for taking pity, man." Knox doubled over as the treadmill came to a stop, his hands braced on his knees.

"It was a solid workout." That wasn't a lie. It just wasn't as strenuous as his usual, that's all.

"I feel about as steady as the goop in that smoothie we

had earlier. And yet there are parts of me screaming that I forgot I had." Knox stood mostly straight then. "Mind if I tag along with you every day? I'd like to see if I can do better."

"With that attitude, I'm sure you will." Marcus nodded. "Of course you're welcome to."

And realistically, they might as well be attached. Marcus was going to be Knox's shadow the entire time he was living at Shields. The guy grabbed a towel and then chugged some water. When he hobbled a few steps, still hugging his ribs, Marcus asked, "Want to hit the hot tub once your heart rate is back to normal?"

"That might take a year or two, but sure. Yeah." Knox walked a slow circuit around the room, getting his breathing under control.

Marcus hated to suggest it, but it was technically his job to make sure Knox was okay. "Do you need me to call Kennedy down to check out your wound?"

Knox flinched at that. "Nah. It'll be fine. Besides, I don't want her to see me like this. It's bad enough that she knows some of the shit I've been up to."

On their next revolution around the gym, they turned toward the pool and spa area. James had really thought of everything when he'd designed and built this place for them. They were spoiled, and Marcus loved it. "There's an actual hot tub, but I'd recommend the jetted cool water version instead. Heat applied in the recovery period after a workout makes it harder for your body to attain parasympathetic activation."

"I have no idea what that means, but yeah. Sure." Knox looked around the area with wide eyes.

"It's not too shabby, huh?" Marcus was proud of the Shields and how they'd grown the business, allowing them to do more good...even if how they achieved those end results often required doing bad things to bad people.

"Not at all, but...where are the dressing rooms? Are there spare suits somewhere?"

"There are towels." Marcus tossed him one off a giant pile of clean laundry. "But to be honest, most of us opt for skinny dipping when we aren't swimming laps or haven't come down here to soak and read a book or whatever on our days off."

"It's not like you haven't already seen my junk." Knox shrugged and dropped his shorts in a single motion.

9

Not to be outdone, Marcus shed his shorts too, eager to get under the cover of the bubbling surface of the spa before his dick decided it wasn't as exhausted as the rest of his body. It still hadn't fully recovered from what he'd witnessed the day before or the dreams he'd been so rudely awakened from earlier.

Knox's bare ass was even paler than the rest of him, inspiring a chuckle from Marcus as he finished stripping and took up a spot on the opposite side of the spa. Damn if the jets didn't feel incredible massaging his back and ass. This had been a great idea.

"Are you laughing at me?" Knox glared even as he sank gingerly into the frothing water. Fortunately, it didn't quite reach the gash in his chest. Kennedy probably wouldn't have approved if it had.

"Not the way you think." Marcus shook his head. "Just noticing you could stand to go naked in the sun a bit more."

"And broil my ass? No fucking thank you." Knox huffed, but his gaze lingered on Marcus's bare torso, which was pretty much the opposite end of the spectrum. "I remember one time when I was living on the streets during the summer, not too long before I met Kennedy, I fell asleep in the park. During the day the cops would leave me alone—I could hide in among the rest of the people hanging out on the grass. But I was so fucking tired I slept in the sun all damn day. Got blisters everywhere. Still have a few scars." He pointed to one that was going to seem minor compared to the trail left by the bullet skimming his pecs.

Marcus wasn't heartless. "It sounds like you had it rough growing up. I'm sorry."

"Not your fault." Knox shrugged one shoulder, then sighed as he relaxed against the jets, letting them massage the soreness from his muscles.

"No, but I recognize that I got lucky in the family lottery and I wish everyone could say the same." Marcus smiled softly as he thought about his mom and dad.

"Tell me about them." Knox wasn't high pressure. Hell, he didn't even have his eyes open.

Marcus was proud of his family and he didn't mind sharing. "My mom is a kickass intellectual property lawyer, and my dad owns an independent pharmacy. They've been together since they were in eighth grade and they worked their butts off to make sure that my sister and I had everything we needed and then some growing up. Most of all, their love. They supported me when I went to school for criminal justice and afterward when I got disillusioned by how broken the system I was supposed to be upholding turned out to be. I got in trouble for saying so a little too loudly on the force, and when Jordan heard about my case, he approached me to come work for Shields, where we might sometimes break the rules, but for all the right reasons. My fam doesn't know exactly what we're up to, but they are smart enough to know this isn't a simple security firm. And somehow they're still proud of me. My mom said she has plenty of lawyer friends if I ever need them to get one of us out of a bind."

"So you're vigilantes?" Knox wondered.

"I guess. Kind of. We operate in a gray area. Sanctioned and hired by official agencies to do what they can't when there's too much red tape tying their hands. At the very least, they look the other way and drop us intel breadcrumbs that lead us to messy situations we can clean up." Marcus sank deeper into the water, letting it wash away the memories of some of the threats he'd eliminated. It wasn't that he liked killing people, it was that sometimes doing so was better than letting them keep hurting innocent people. He didn't regret it. And if that made him a psychopath, well, so be it.

"At least there's a code of honor to what you're doing." Knox rested his head on the edge of the spa. "Where I came from, everyone was scrambling to survive and if that meant you dragged someone else down to get ahead..."

"Is that how you got mixed up with the Vipers?" Marcus asked. He couldn't believe Kennedy would have involved herself with him if he'd already been headed down that path.

Knox let out a harsh laugh. "Nah. Actually was trying to do the right thing too. But it didn't work out. I was destined to be gutter trash."

"What does that mean?" Marcus sat up straighter, not that Knox noticed with his eyes still scrunched as if he could block out the memories.

"I was seventeen when I fell for Kennedy. Believed the stuff she told me about how we could make a better future for ourselves. And that things didn't have to be like they'd turned out for my mom. So when I got approached by some undercover cop to be a mole, and bring them some evidence as a kind of tryout for their program, I took it."

Marcus didn't interrupt, afraid Knox might clam up at the slightest hint of judgment.

"The problem was that to get what he needed, I had to fit in. I had to be one of them, at least for a while. I didn't think it would be an issue. Buy a little from them, smoke it with them a time or two until I could get everything the cops needed on my wire. Problem is, from the very first hit...it changed my life. It was magical poison. When I was high, none of my problems mattered. I had never felt so light. Except maybe when I was with Kennedy, though then I was worried constantly she was going to figure out that I didn't belong with her. I also had some attraction to dudes, and I didn't know how to tell her. If she would take it the right way or freak out or think it changed how I felt about her. We were young. And I was an idiot. Still am, mostly."

Marcus forced himself to stay planted where he was. "You were an addict with no support—that's not the same thing at all."

"Yeah, well, that's not what the cops said. Once they had what they needed from me, they didn't reward me with an admissions letter to the academy like they'd promised. Nope, they threatened to toss my ass in jail. *That's* why I had to leave. And the only option I had, and —let's be honest, the only way I could score more drugs— was hustling for the Vipers in exchange for a place to go. No way was I about to get Kennedy tangled up in that shit. So I bailed. On her, on the future we'd pretended could be real. On myself. For a long time. I don't remember a lot of it to be honest. I was so fucked up, in a lot of ways."

"So what turned things around?" Marcus figured Knox was a hell of a lot stronger than he gave himself credit for. To have survived all that. To have slipped through every crack in the system as a child and to have been let down by an institution he should have been able to trust, exactly like Marcus had...

It was a lot.

"Maybe we've been in here long enough." Knox pushed up a bit, water sluicing down his flat abdomen, but Marcus lunged forward and clamped his hand on Knox's wrist.

"Not yet. Look, it's obvious to me that Kennedy disagrees with your assessment of yourself. She's never gotten over you. So tell me why I should let you be around her now and how you're different, and definitely not going to hurt her again."

"Oh, so that's why you gave me this shiner, huh? You have a hard-on for her too?" Knox shook his head as if pitying Marcus. "Of course you do—who wouldn't? You saw how she rode me yesterday. Damn."

Now neither of them were getting out of the spa any time soon.

They settled back in, Marcus willing his dick not to respond to the echo of Kennedy's moans ringing through his mind. "She's magnificent. You saw her in the field. She's confident and incredible at her job. She has this way of calming people down when they're injured and fixing them even in shitty conditions so they can do it all over again another day. She's smart as fuck, funny, and...well... wounded down deep. It's a combination that's impossible to resist."

"You forgot drop-dead gorgeous," Knox offered.

"That too." Marcus didn't bother denying it, though it was only one of many things he found irresistibly attractive about her.

"You ever made a move on her?" Knox asked with a wicked tip to one side of his mouth.

"Kissed her last night." Marcus couldn't resist a tiny jab. He was still a guy, after all.

"But did you fuck her?" Knox was pushing his luck now.

"Don't make me give you a matching black eye," Marcus growled.

"I'm taking that as a no. Noted." Knox full-on grinned.

"That's your fault, asshole. You broke her so bad she doesn't let anyone else in." Marcus groaned.

"I didn't ask about her heart. I asked if you slept with her." Knox scrubbed a hand over his face. "Anyway, don't worry. I never had before yesterday either. And I wouldn't say that was a stellar performance."

They both knew Knox hadn't even come though he'd gotten Kennedy off more than once.

Knox sobered then. "Of course, I'd pretty much sworn off sex myself since I seem to ruin the lives of everyone around me. And to answer your question, what happened... I guess I got pretty good at doing whatever the Vipers needed done in exchange for drugs and a shithole to exist in while high. They kept giving me more elaborate jobs and bigger payoffs. Eventually I got hooked up with a guy named Riggs, the nephew of Vex, who's the head of the gang. We, uh, were more than friends. Lovers. But when I scored some of this hardcore hybrid shit as payment for one of my errands, he didn't believe the rumors about how strong it was. Both of us thought we could handle it."

Marcus clenched his hands on the tile bench he was sitting on as if it could prevent what he knew was coming. Poor bastard. "He OD'd?"

"We both did." Knox stared right at Marcus then, with the most haunted gaze he'd ever seen. "But for some reason, they were able to bring me back. Not him."

"Fuck," Marcus hissed. "I'm so sorry."

"I don't know. It might have been a lot easier to go out on a high like that. I'm sure he didn't feel any pain." Knox threw one arm over his face as if too embarrassed or ashamed to meet Marcus's horrified stare.

It was then Marcus realized precisely how lost Knox was and how desperately he might need a bright light like Kennedy to help him find his way back to a life filled with something other than backstabbing, misery, and suffering.

"Is that why you tried to commit suicide by informing?" Marcus asked quietly.

"Maybe." Knox shrugged one shoulder, the one farthest from his injury, which seemed even more terrifying now that Marcus realized how little Knox cared for himself. No wonder he'd been willing to fling himself in front of the Viper for Kennedy. "Or maybe I wanted a shot at doing one good thing before I'm used up."

"Well, you definitely have the opportunity to do that now, by helping us shut them down." Marcus believed now that Knox might be the key Jordan had thought he would be all along.

Knox nodded.

Marcus cleared his throat. There was only one more thing he really wanted to ask. "Did Kennedy ever find out you're bisexual?"

Marcus couldn't help prying. Because as far as he knew, she'd had no clue that he was sometimes attracted to men too, even if he'd never found one he'd wanted to act on those impulses with before.

"Nope." Knox frowned. "Hell, I didn't fully admit it to myself until Riggs swallowed my cock for the first time. Even then I played it off as something I only did when I was high and not thinking straight for a lot longer than I should have. I wonder if I'd acknowledged what we really had, if Riggs wouldn't have been so eager to avoid his own struggles by taking so much shit that night."

"You should definitely take Jordan up on counseling sessions." Marcus tried to be gentle when he suggested it.

"I'm not sure there's enough time left in any of our lives to hash out all my issues, but hey, what the fuck. Trying new things. Why not?" Knox pinched the bridge of his nose and then winced as he mashed the bruise there.

"Sorry about that black eye." Marcus felt a smidge bad about it now.

"I deserved it. That and a million more." Knox did climb from the spa then, wrapping a towel around his waist with two flicks of his wrists.

"For the record, you don't need to worry around the Shields." Marcus got out too, fully aware of Knox's gaze glued to his crotch as he toweled off. "Whether you're bi, poly, straight, ace, whatever, we've pretty much seen and embraced it all within our group."

"Seriously? Some of those guys didn't seem like they'd be the tolerant type." Knox shot Marcus some side-eye.

"Well, considering Jordan has both a husband and a wife, and Nolan's got a girlfriend and a boyfriend, and Ransom and Levi are partners outside of the office plus go home to the same wife, and James...jeez. He's got a husband, a wife, and six other best friends, whom he hooks up with, and will be more than happy to explicitly detail those encounters for you, unintentionally rubbing in the fact that you don't even have a single lover.... Yeah."

"Are you shitting me right now?" Knox seemed skeptical.

"Nope." Marcus shrugged. "I guess Middletown is a hotbed of sexual open-mindedness these days. You have nothing to worry about."

"Huh." Knox seemed to slouch a little less then. He turned toward Marcus and sighed. "Thanks. You didn't have to be cool with me. Especially since I ruined your chances with Kennedy. I'll try to make things right."

"Maybe you should let me worry about my chances with the people I'm interested in." Marcus couldn't say what possessed him—maybe it was the confused look in Knox's gaze, like he didn't know what to do with people who weren't out to screw him over—but he found himself taking a step forward and wrapping his hand around the back of Knox's neck.

And just like he had with Kennedy the night before, he ignored his better sense, dipping his head to deliver a short, hard, but thorough kiss to Knox's lips, which were parted in utter shock.

It only took a fraction of a second before the other guy groaned then kissed him back. But before it had hardly begun, Marcus broke them apart, his cock tenting his towel. When he looked down, Knox's cheeks turned red.

Marcus chuckled but didn't object when Knox turned and marched toward the elevators. They rode in silence up to his floor and on the short walk to his door. Once inside, as if by tacit agreement, they each went to their separate rooms, and shut their doors.

With only one wall between them, Marcus had no doubt that Knox was relieving more tension than the spa had by jerking off when his soft grunts and groans filtered through the drywall. So Marcus did the same, taking his shaft in hand and pumping. It took embarrassingly few strokes as he thought about watching his *two* obsessions fucking the day before, the conversation he'd just had with Knox, and the way Kennedy and Knox's lips felt pressed to his before he launched his release across his chest with a roar he couldn't have smothered if he'd tried.

Knox's answering cry reverberated through Marcus's nerve endings, setting off aftershocks that puddled the last of his come on his abdomen. As he imagined Knox cleaning himself up and what it would be like if they showered together, along with Kennedy, instead of separately, Marcus realized they were fucked.

Because sometime...sometime soon...they were going to have to face Kennedy and the intense and twisted connections strung between the three of them.

10

———

Kennedy clutched the folder containing Knox's test results to her chest as if it was plate armor instead of simple paper. Given what they'd done the day before, she had a vested interest in the contents. It hadn't felt right to read them before Knox, though.

So she was going to have to put on her big girl panties and face him. The night before, she'd spent hours rehashing and processing everything that had happened, so quickly, that day. And then some quality time with her arsenal of toys. Every time she thought about how damn good Knox had made her feel while Marcus was spying on them, she got horny again.

Damn them both.

She'd avoided the guys all morning by spending time advocating for Ace at the hospital and overseeing his eventual release. He was settled as comfortably as possible in his apartment with Liam hovering over him. Which meant she was officially out of excuses.

Fortunately, she didn't have a long trek to dread

encountering Marcus and Knox or even far enough to go to change her mind. She stepped out of her apartment and knocked on Marcus's door. For the past month, she'd loved knowing he was so close. Now, she wasn't sure what to think.

"Hey, come on in." Marcus didn't seem upset to see her. He ushered her down the entry hall that mirrored hers and into his living room. They'd chosen a lot of the same finishes, which ordinarily made her feel as at home in his place as she did in her own. Not with both him and Knox staring at her, though. "How's Ace?"

"Pissed off that he's going to have to sit on the sidelines for a few months. Bitching about doing rehab and therapy."

"Ah, so he's fine, you mean?" Marcus grinned.

"His ulna is sporting some spiffy new titanium hardware. He'll live, but it's not going to be a fun recovery." She was surprised when she caught Knox's wince.

"So him and that giant blond guy attached to his hip probably already hate me, huh?" Knox planted his elbow on his knee and put his face in his hand. "I don't blame them."

Marcus looked at her with wide eyes as if imploring her to do something about Knox's beaten attitude. Like what? Fuck him again?

Ugh! How was *she* going to survive with them both making her crazy?

"You're not the one who shot him. You were otherwise occupied." Kennedy figured reminding him would either cheer him up or aggravate him, considering she'd intended to manipulate him.

He lifted his face and speared her with a scorching

gaze. Well, at least she wasn't the only one suffering. At least she'd come. How embarrassing that she hadn't even finished the job.

"Speaking of that...I have your test results." She held the folder out to him. He didn't reach for it, acting as if it was a real live snake.

"Just tell me. Am I okay? Are you?" His face seemed to go ghost white.

"I don't know. It's your information." She shook the papers a bit.

"You didn't look? It matters to you too. I mean, we used protection, but..."

"I'm trying not to invade your privacy, but maybe you should check and let me know if there's anything I need to be concerned about." Kennedy pressed the folder a bit closer and this time he took it. Knox surprised her by looking to Marcus, who seemed to lend his encouragement with a slight nod.

What the hell was that about?

Marcus was a decent man. Had he taken Knox in like a stray dog? How could she resist him when he was sexy *and* so damn nice?

Knox flipped open the folder and thumbed through his results. His sigh was audible even from several feet away when he reached the end of the paperwork. "I have no idea how, but...looks like I'm healthy."

"Why were you worried? Because of sharing needles?" She hated to think of him in the grips of his addiction.

"I'm pretty sure I didn't do that much. But maybe, if I was desperate enough or too high and drunk to give a shit. But, uh, I wasn't safe with my last lover, who was also an addict and part of the Vipers." He stared at his bare feet, his toes curled in Marcus's plush silver rug. It accented the comfortable modern style of the whole place and was incredibly soft, as she knew from the times she'd done the same while watching a movie or decompressing after a mission.

Kennedy realized she was distracting herself from the burst of possessiveness that hit her at the thought of him sleeping with someone else. Of course, he'd probably had plenty of relationships since theirs. She was the only dumbass she knew who clung to a dead end for a decade.

"Oh. Well, if you want some way to share the news with her, I'll see what Ruby can arrange without giving your location away." Kennedy tried to maintain a professional tone.

"Not necessary." Knox groaned and Marcus winced. Did he already know about Knox's recent affairs? "*He* is dead."

"Oh my God. Please tell me he wasn't one of the guys we took out yesterday." Kennedy's hand flew to her mouth. Had they killed Knox's lover? And if so, what had he been doing screwing her?

"You're more worried about hurting someone I care about than the fact that I just told you I'm bi?" He tipped his head.

"What the hell kind of judgmental monster do you think I am?" She propped her hand on her hip.

"I always knew you were far better than I deserved," Knox muttered as he rubbed his chest, then winced. "I ruin things for everyone eventually. And no. Riggs overdosed a few months ago. So did I. On that new shit you confiscated yesterday. I haven't touched it since. If you'd told me that day I could sit on a fucking mountain of it and not sample a bit, I'd have laughed in your face.

But it made me sick to even be near it. All I could see was his blank stare when I looked at those bricks."

"Ah, fuck." Marcus leaned in as if he wanted to comfort Knox but held back, as unsure of what to do as Kennedy was.

"I'm so sorry, Knox." And she was. No one should have to lose someone they loved. The debilitating pain could haunt you forever. As much as his presence was sure to turn her life upside down again, she was grateful he'd survived such a close call. Probably one of many he'd had since they'd parted. "And glad you're still here."

"Hmm." He didn't sound as thrilled about it. "All I've ever done is hurt the few people who gave a shit about me." Knox stood then and crossed to her.

"Is that why you disappeared? Did you realize you wanted a man instead of me?" She cleared her suddenly raw throat. "You could have told me. I would have understood."

"Kennedy, no." He put his hand on the side of her neck, making her jump and Marcus hover protectively. "That just sort of...happened. We were friends first. Partners. Got into and out of so much shit we thought we must be invincible. And when we used, it seemed like we could be. He made the first move, and I told myself at first I only went through with it because I was stoned. But it wasn't true. It was more than that. He always had my back, and when he was gone...but I was still here..."

He shrugged, and she couldn't remain unmoved. Kennedy hugged him carefully, laying her head on his shoulder, which left her staring at Marcus. Instead of being furious, he flashed her a soft smile.

"Maybe I should give you two some space." Marcus

shuffled toward his bedroom. "Are you comfortable with that, Kennedy?"

"No."

Knox stiffened in her hold.

"I mean, I don't want you to leave, Marcus." She didn't trust herself enough to be responsible if she was left alone with Knox.

"I haven't given you any reason to believe me, but I would never hurt you, Kennedy. Not like that. Not on purpose. And I regret that I already have. I've cursed the day I agreed to work with the cops and how fucked up everything got after that."

"Wait. What?" Kennedy stepped back so she could stare into his mesmerizing eyes. "What do you mean?"

"Your boy here was a mole. But when he did what they asked of him and ended up addicted to drugs, the cops fucking abandoned him in that hellhole. I had James reach out to JRad and verify his records. Knox is telling the truth."

Kennedy whipped her gaze from Knox to Marcus and back. Marcus must have known it would be nearly impossible for her to trust Knox again. He'd checked for her sake. Even though he knew how she felt about Knox and that finding this out would only bring them closer.

"You did what?" Knox glared. "I thought you believed me."

"I did. In this business, I also like to double check my gut whenever possible." Marcus shrugged, clearly trying to smooth things over. "I think you'll agree, in our line of work there's not a lot you can take on faith."

Knox took a deep breath. "Okay, fair enough."

"So like I said, if you need some privacy..." Marcus pivoted.

"No." This time Knox and Kennedy said it simultaneously. They looked at each other and then back to the man who seemed to make the perfect buffer for them both.

Marcus returned to the living room, inviting them to sink onto the sofa while he faced them in an armchair.

"If I had known..." Kennedy rubbed her temples, trying to make sense of what he was telling her.

"There wasn't much you could have done." Knox spoke softly, as if from far away as he remembered that time in his life. "It started with the bust going off the rails, but I got sucked into the organization pretty quickly. I don't know, maybe it felt good to have somebody tell me I didn't suck at something for once, even if that something was something horrible—selling drugs, screwing over other people just like myself, getting in fights to protect our turf and keep our sales up. You know, whatever it took to keep the praise and the drugs coming, and gave me a built-in family, even if it was a fucked up one. They took me in, made me feel like I belonged somewhere for the first time."

"What about me? Didn't I make you feel that way?" Kennedy still hated that she had failed so miserably when it came to him.

"You tried, but I couldn't believe it. Not when I felt like such shit about myself. My own mother didn't love me, and she was a screw up. How could someone as intelligent, funny, and so damn....*together* as you care? And then once I worked for the Vipers, I knew you'd never want me back. Not after everything I did. I tried to show you I still cared from a distance whenever I was sober for long enough and didn't think it would put you in jeopardy."

"What do you mean?" Kennedy whispered, because in her heart, she already knew.

"Did you think it was just some random coincidence that you'd find violets in your path every once in a while? Planted in the beds outside your apartment, or in the park you jogged in, stuff like that." Knox wondered.

Marcus leaned forward as if watching some tragic movie unfold.

"I thought I was imagining it and that it was coincidental." Kennedy recalled at least a half dozen other examples. The window boxes outside her college lab. Around the bench she'd taken her breaks at in the courtyard of the hospital where she'd done her residency. "They always reminded me of you, but I had no idea you were putting them where I'd come across them. That thought never even occurred to me."

"Does it creep you out now that you know?" He grimaced. "Riggs used to make fun of me so bad and call me a stalker."

"Not in the least. Though it kind of pisses me off you never even said hello." Kennedy's soul twisted as she realized he'd been sending her messages that whole time. Trying to tell her he still cared. She'd cried over the memories those flowers surfaced within her, kept a few pressed between the pages of her anatomy books, and thought she was ridiculous for remembering a young man who'd left her without a backward glance.

"Then I probably shouldn't mention that I was there to see you graduate from med school. I loved the purple dress you wore under your gown. You looked incredible." Knox sighed.

"*That's* why you weren't surprised when I told you I was a doctor in the bar yesterday?" She reeled as she considered how near he'd been on those special occasions that she'd missed him most.

He nodded.

"That's romantic as shit. You should kiss him for that," Marcus said as if that wasn't weird given their relationship and how they'd done the same the evening before. "I can see you want to. Don't let me stop you."

"Oh yeah?" Kennedy raised a brow. She looked to Marcus, who nodded subtly. How did he not only totally get her but also approve? She wasn't going to second-guess herself. In the moment, it felt right. So she did as he'd suggested and angled her head toward Knox.

Their lips were a hairsbreadth apart as she stared into his eyes. He'd been so far astray and she hadn't had a clue that he needed her to find him. Yet somehow, fate had brought them back together. And she didn't intend to waste that chance.

"Before you do that—" Knox drew back, tripping Kennedy's anxieties about whether or not he was serious or would simply rip her heart in half again if she gave him the opportunity.

"What?" Her eyes narrowed.

"I don't want to make the same mistakes as last time. I owe you the entire truth." His gaze flicked guiltily toward Marcus.

"What the hell is happening here?" Kennedy stared at one, then the other.

"I sort of kissed your man. And I'm not even going to apologize for it." Knox shrugged. "I liked it."

Kennedy was glad she was sitting or she would have fallen straight onto her ass. "You did what?"

"Kissed Marcus when we were skinny-dipping in the Jacuzzi downstairs."

"I was only gone for like four hours." Kennedy couldn't help it—she laughed. Was it hysteria taking over or did she really find the idea of the two of them together both hot and somehow amusing in its complete outrageousness?

"Are you mad?" Marcus asked.

"Did you enjoy it?" she countered.

"Uh, yup." He toyed with the diamond stud in his ear, one of the very few tells he had.

"Holy crap. Even you're not immune to his bullshit charm." Kennedy's jaw hung open. In a weird way it made her feel better about how much she still craved Knox, even after how much had happened between them and the time that had separated them.

Then a sinking feeling overcame her. "Hang on. Maybe it's me who should give you two some privacy."

She rocked forward, about to stand, when Knox put his hand on her thigh and kept her pinned to the couch beside him. "It just happened, Kennedy. I'm in a weird place. My whole world is changing and I see a way out where I thought there wasn't any chance of escape. Then throw you in the mix. And now your guy here and... I don't know. Everything seems like it's moving really fast right now. But I know it feels more right than anything has in a long time."

"You really trust him?" Kennedy asked Marcus, glad to have an unbiased opinion. "He's telling the truth, about all of it?"

Marcus took his time really considering, then nodded. "Yeah, I believe so."

"So you're not mad? Or freaked out? Or whatever?" Knox picked at his chewed fingernails.

How had she never realized his teenaged confidence

had been a bluff? Maybe if she'd realized he wasn't the arrogant player she'd assumed, things could have turned out differently.

"I'm not upset. You don't owe me anything. Either of you." It hurt to admit it. She'd turned Marcus down enough times that it was too late to stake a claim now. And if he ended up with Knox instead of her, it would be her own damn fault for pushing him away because she was too scared to let herself be vulnerable.

And now she was in the impossible position of having feelings for two men and being unable to choose between them. Which only meant she was going to end up crushing someone, probably all three of them, to be honest.

"Well, I guess what I'm wondering is...what do you want, Kennedy?" Marcus reached across the gap between them and squeezed her hand. It seemed so small enveloped in his heat and strength. "It's not a matter of obligation. We both want you, so it's up to you. If you pick him, I'll back off. Because all I really care about is your happiness."

Knox swallowed hard and agreed, "If I'm going to fuck your life up again, I'll walk away."

"Not with the Vipers hunting you." Kennedy shook her head.

Marcus had her back, as usual. "If you bail, I'll get fired. You don't want to cost me my career, do you?"

Knox groaned. "Okay, fine. You know what I mean, though."

Kennedy was frozen between them, poised at a juncture in her life she didn't think she'd ever arrive at again. What if she made the wrong decision? She looked at Knox, swearing she could see his mislaid soul searching for even the slightest bit of acceptance, then Marcus, who had always been steady and dependable. Everything she'd needed to feel safe and secure. If she could give a little of that back to him, shouldn't she? Simply because he didn't need her like Knox did, didn't mean he didn't deserve to have what he wanted.

Kennedy leaned in and kissed Knox, figuring it was her way of saying goodbye. One more taste, one bittersweet glide of her lips over his to allow them to part, maybe as friends this time. That's not how it turned out, though. Because the instant they connected, sparks flew. They stared into each other's eyes as they shared the agony they'd both endured and gave it an outlet. They turned their pain into something beautiful, something Marcus didn't seem to mind watching. He stared at them, shifting in his seat to rearrange his stiffening cock.

And when Knox noticed her diverted attention, he broke their kiss with a sad smile. "I don't blame you in the least, Kennedy. Go ahead. He deserves you."

Marcus seemed shocked when she rose. He mimicked her and so did Knox. The three of them stood there, awfully close, as she left Knox's arms and went into Marcus's. She sighed as she raised onto her tiptoes to kiss him, feeling like she was coming home. And if she hoped it made Knox even a sliver as green-eyed as she'd been to hear of his lover and his stolen kiss with Marcus, well... she'd never said she was perfect.

As Marcus looped his arms around her and pressed his tongue into her mouth, swiping along her own and making her hungrier than ever for his touch, she understood clearly why so many of her friends like James, Jordan, and Nolan enjoyed sharing their partners and being shared by them in return.

If she'd been attracted to Marcus and Knox individually, the power of their desire was amplified by the presence of each other. Instead of twice as arousing, together they seemed ten times so. Maybe that was because they were making her feel so damn good about herself. Powerful enough to take care of them both if only she could let go of her fears and her hangups and take what they were so generously offering.

Marcus removed one hand from her lower back and used it to snag Knox. He dragged the other man closer yet, then allowed his lips to slip away from hers long enough to show her exactly what she'd missed earlier. Watching the guys make out from a centimeter away didn't repulse her. Instead it turned her on. That must have accounted for her boldness. She joined them, pressing her mouth to the corners of theirs until they groaned and made room for her in what became a three-way kiss.

It was only when it was replenish her oxygen supply or pass out that Kennedy reluctantly broke their exchange. She gulped in air as she studied their flushed faces and the equally erratic pulses pounding in their carotid arteries. Could it be that whatever they were about to do meant as much to them as it did to her?

Knox laughed ruefully. "You know, Riggs used to get annoyed with me for telling the same old stories about you all the time. But really, I think it irritated him most that I couldn't move on. It means something to me that you never got over me, because I sure as hell never stopped loving you."

"Yeah, well, I'm pretty sure you never forget the guy who took your virginity." Kennedy snorted. "So you're good for life."

"Look, I was messed up back then, especially when

shit started to unravel. We fooled around plenty, making out and me sneaking some handfuls of your boobs. But I'm sure I would remember if we'd actually had sex. My dick had never been inside you until yesterday."

"Trust me, I'm painfully aware of the timing." Kennedy rolled her eyes.

"Wait." Marcus stood up straight, his lazy grace vanishing in an instant. "Are you saying you were a virgin before this mission?"

Kennedy simply shrugged.

"And you let *that* be your first time?" He slammed his eyes closed.

Knox cursed. "For fuck's sake, I didn't even undress you!"

"Didn't need to, apparently." Kennedy tried to act like it was no big deal. "You got me off faster than even my favorite vibrator. Which is pretty impressive given that I aced anatomy and I could stock an entire store with the toys I've taken care of myself with all this time."

"Are you hearing this?" Knox turned to Marcus, exasperated.

"Uh huh." The gold flecks in Marcus's irises nearly seemed to glow as his stare intensified.

"And are you thinking we should show her something nicer than a quickie in some rundown shack?" Knox put his hand around her waist, keeping her in place as Marcus advanced, sandwiching her between them.

"Fuck yes." Marcus leaned in and nuzzled her neck, making her shudder. "Let us treat you right, Kennedy. With both of us concentrating on you, it'll be worth all this time you've waited."

Kennedy realized this was probably going to come back to bite her later, but in that moment she felt like being selfish. Greedy. Both of the men she'd ever lusted after were within reach and willing to share this special occasion with her.

She'd waited practically forever. Faced with a double helping of temptation, there was no way she was going to deny herself this opportunity to finally experience lovemaking the way she'd held out for. Because while it might be just sex for them, Kennedy knew the men she was surrounded by were the only two who would ever hold her heart, even if she didn't intend to admit it—not even to herself and certainly not to them.

"Okay. Yes. Let's do it." Kennedy flung her arms around Marcus's neck when he scooped her into his arms and marched toward his bedroom with Knox one step behind.

11

Knox was starting to wonder if he'd really taken a bullet to the heart in the woods and this was what heaven was like. A continuation of your previous life but one where everything suddenly started to go right. Probably not since he'd have gone to hell for all the fucked up shit he'd done.

But this... This was one chance he had to fix some of his mistakes and have a lot of fun while doing it.

Hanging out at Shields, even for a day, had given him ideas it would be better to forget. Otherwise he might start to think he really could work toward becoming the person he'd always wished he was, even if he constantly disappointed himself. The cost of failure was so steep that for a moment he craved something to take the edge off. It was a vicious circle.

Knox reminded himself he could achieve an even more potent high by losing himself in Kennedy and concentrating on her pleasure. Doing that might even distract him from his own struggles.

He glanced over at Marcus, who cradled Kennedy to his

chest as he carried her into his bedroom. Her platinum hair cascaded across the other man's dark skin. They were both beautiful and so damn strong, in completely opposite ways.

Weird as it might be, Knox was grateful to have Marcus there. His level head and ironclad self-control were something Knox would never be able to achieve. No matter what, Marcus wouldn't get carried away—he wouldn't let Knox torment Kennedy again. Unless it was in the best possible way.

Knox shucked his shirt and glanced at Marcus, who nodded, before climbing onto the other guy's bed. He held out his arms and Marcus placed Kennedy in them. She rotated, letting go of Marcus and clinging to him instead. How? How could she trust him even enough to spend one single afternoon together?

It wasn't the smartest thing she'd ever done, but he wasn't honorable enough to argue about it. If this was what she wanted, he was more than willing to teach her about how incredible sex could be. And he suspected he'd never experienced passion as they were about to, the three of them, together.

Knox brushed a kiss over Kennedy's forehead, then a chain of them down her nose and cheek, before grazing her lips, which were already flushed from their three-way exchange. "I thought I'd missed the chance to share this with you. Thank you for giving me another shot."

"It feels right." Kennedy peeked up at Marcus, who was getting rid of his own shirt, peeling the charcoal-gray cotton off his ripped muscles, revealing exactly how much work he put in at the gym. Damn. Forget six-pack, the man had eight abs at least. "Especially like this. I've spent too long being apprehensive about letting go..."

"I didn't help, huh?" Knox grimaced. "I'm so sorry—"

"You've already apologized, and a lot of it wasn't your fault." Kennedy stretched up to kiss him gently, soothing him with tender licks across his lips. "It's done. It's gone. All we can do is get it right now."

How could she be so gracious? Knox's hang-ups kept him from realizing at first that she was asking for forgiveness too, in her own way, from Marcus. For holding him at arm's length for too long. Damn. Maybe they weren't as perfect as they seemed to be from his perspective. Maybe they really did need him too, just a little.

"Well, there's no reason to be nervous, okay?" Knox remembered how worked up she'd get over a test she was guaranteed to nail or about being at least five minutes early for every appointment. There were things he hadn't understood back then, which he could see more clearly now, and the way they'd wound each other up was one of them.

"If you want to stop at any time, just say so. No hard feelings." Marcus chuckled as he said it, glancing down at the impressive bulge in his jeans and then to Knox's crotch. "We already know Knox won't die if you leave him hanging."

Kennedy snorted and covered her face with her hand. "I can't believe I did that."

"You didn't exactly have a choice since we were so rudely interrupted. But I'm so glad you at least let me take care of you and I swear, that was only a tiny sample of what it could be like. Let me do this right." Knox brushed her hair back from her forehead, and when she revealed her bright blue eyes and stunning smile to him again, he dipped down for a taste of the sunshine that radiated from within her.

"Yesterday was kind of like breaking the ice." Kennedy sighed. "It's technically done already, so there's no reason I can't just enjoy today."

"You damn well better." Marcus's voice seemed even deeper than usual as he joined them.

Knox settled Kennedy on the neat steel-gray comforter and plush pillows. He held her hand as Marcus stretched out beside her and rolled onto his side so they were eye to eye. With her free hand, Kennedy reached up and drew a wavy line along the shaved part of Marcus's hair. He wondered how long she'd been wanting to do that.

"You have no idea how many times I almost walked across this hall to beg you to do this with me." Kennedy glided the pad of her thumb over his bottom lip, making Knox's dick jerk in his pants.

"I would have. In a second." Marcus opened his mouth and sucked her thumb inside, nibbling on it.

"I know. That's why I was so afraid." Kennedy closed her eyes briefly and swallowed. "We can't let this fuck up work stuff. The Shields are all I have."

"You have me," Marcus promised.

"And me, for as long as you want me," Knox added. If it was only for this one magical moment, he'd still be grateful they'd included him.

"I swear to you, nothing we do today will impact our relationship on the job." Marcus genuinely believed that, even Knox could see it in his stare, but that didn't mean it was true. "And if it did, I would leave."

"No." Kennedy hooked her hand around his neck and

drew him close. "You're my partner and I wouldn't feel as safe with anyone else."

"That means everything to me." Marcus rested his forehead on hers.

"You're really okay with this?" Kennedy glanced at Knox. "I'm sorry it didn't happen before, when it was only you and me."

"Do you want me to go?" Knox understood. He was a novelty. They could have something lasting. He wasn't such a bastard that he'd want them to sacrifice forever for an afternoon of fun.

Both Kennedy and Marcus responded, "No."

"Maybe this is how it was always meant to be." Marcus reached across Kennedy and wrapped one of his broad hands around Knox's wrist, tugging him so that he landed beside them. The manacle his fingers made did nothing to make Knox less aroused. "You and I are both too cautious. Maybe we needed a push, a wild card to get us moving in the right direction."

Knox thought that was a nice way of putting it. They were stable. He constantly imploded. For once, he wished he could get it together and be more like them. The only way he could think to express himself was to show them how much he admired them.

"Less talking. More kissing." He nipped Kennedy's earlobe before stretching out along the full length of her and claiming her mouth.

She practically purred between his parted lips, moaning when he slipped his tongue inside and toyed with hers. Then he backed off and nudged her chin to the side, offering Marcus a turn. He couldn't say how long they spent lying there, enjoying the simple pleasure of learning each other's responses and seeing which man could turn her on the most.

Eventually, he moved beyond her mouth, licking her neck, sucking gently and raking his teeth below her ear when Marcus was taking his turn tasting her lips. The other guy did the same on her other side, murmuring reassurance in her ear in between sensual caresses.

It was slow and shockingly easy. As if they had eternity, not only this short intermission before the Vipers tracked him down and got their revenge.

No, he wasn't going to think about that now. Wasn't going to worry or sabotage what was undoubtedly going to be the best moment of his life. Knox ran his fingers through the silk of Kennedy's hair. He traced the ball of her shoulder, then slid downward until he could lace his fingers with hers.

She held on tight and so did he.

"I wish we'd had a chance to plan," Marcus grumbled. "I would have done something more romantic. Gotten flowers or some candles or something."

"That's not real life." Kennedy shook her head.

Knox winced. It should have been for her. He could have made it happen all those years ago, but he'd been too young, too lost, to know better. He had more in common with a villain than a prince at this point, but he intended to do his best to make their time together fairytale-worthy.

"For today, it's your reality," Marcus promised.

"So far you two are all talk and no action." Kennedy pouted, clearly ready to move to the next level.

Knox couldn't help it—he grinned. She was adorable when she was horny. He teased, "You don't like kissing?"

"Don't act like that's enough for you." She rolled her eyes.

But the weird thing was, Knox got more pleasure from kissing her than he had from fucking...or being fucked... in the past. Being inside her had been sweet torture and he wasn't sure how long he'd be able to last this time around. So for now, it was plenty.

Marcus indulged her impatience, though. He slid his hand beneath her sage green tank top with tiny spaghetti straps and spanned her flat stomach, stroking it with a single pass of his huge palm. She gasped and squirmed, leaving Knox to swallow her passion before kissing her some more.

They only paused making out to allow Marcus to peel the thin shirt from her. Knox stole a glance of her small breasts tipped with tight nipples before continuing his exploration. Kennedy reached up, buried her fingers in Knox's hair, and tugged a little as Marcus began to knead her chest.

When Marcus nudged Knox's face aside with his own, Knox took up where the other man had left off, strumming his thumb over the hard peaks of her breasts. The day before, his hands had been bound. Touching her now, the satin of her skin gliding against his rough fingers, made him groan.

"You going to make it?" Marcus looked down with a smirk.

"I hope so." Knox clamped one hand over his rock-hard cock through his jeans, as if that would settle it down. "But I need to taste her."

Marcus looked to Kennedy, who arched off the bed. She wheezed, "Please do."

Knox didn't need to be told twice. He opened his

mouth wide to cover as much of her breast as possible before slowly closing it, dragging his lip-covered teeth over her flesh. And when he had just her nipple in his mouth, he began to suck and lave it with his tongue.

"Oh shit." Kennedy shuddered under him and Marcus, her legs instinctively spreading wider, knocking into both of them where they lounged on either side of her.

Knox petted her svelte abdomen as Marcus took advantage of her distraction to unbutton her jeans and begin working them down her hips. He placed a kiss on every square inch of her skin that he exposed. "She's so beautiful, isn't she?"

"Mmm." Knox wasn't about to release her tit from his mouth long enough to answer with actual words when his agreement was so obvious.

When her pussy, shrouded by pale pink lace underwear, was bared, Marcus nuzzled it, breathing deep but refusing to be distracted before he'd finished undressing her. Instead, he kissed his way down one thigh while massaging the other. Knox shifted to give the opposite side of her chest some attention, pinning her to the bed as Marcus rid her of her jeans and socks.

"Guys, I don't want to be the only one naked here," Kennedy practically squeaked.

As slow and gentle as they were being with her, when she made her request, they fulfilled it immediately. Marcus had to stand and do a few contortions to get his zipper undone without maiming himself given the absolute raging erection he was sporting. His briefs couldn't hide the outline of his dick, which stretched nearly to his hip as it strained the cotton. There was only so much the poor underwear could do to hold him back.

And when he peeled them off, his cock hung thick and heavy, bouncing some, between his muscled thighs.

Knox had the urge to suck it. To take Marcus as deep into his throat as he could manage, but as if by some tacit understanding, he and Marcus opted to make Kennedy the focus of their encounter.

"Damn," Kennedy whispered, snaking her hand toward her pussy as if they were going to make her take care of herself. Old habits died hard, he figured. Then she looked at him. "You too."

"I'm not nearly as impressive." Knox huffed out a self-deprecating laugh.

"Tell that to someone you didn't get off in like ten minutes flat." Kennedy shoved his shoulder and beamed up at him, making him feel as if he had a porn-worthy endowment like Marcus.

Marcus chuckled and stroked himself a few times as Knox rid himself of his clothes. Then he couldn't help jerking his aching cock too. He and Marcus hovered over Kennedy, appreciating every damn bit of her. As if her confidence grew because of their awe, she reached out, knocking their hands aside so she could work their cocks for them.

Marcus broke first, tugging away from her before slipping her panties from her long, long legs. Figured, he wasn't the sort to rip them off like Knox had the day before. But he was definitely the kind of man to make sure his woman was satisfied before he so much as thought of burying himself inside her.

Knox stared as Marcus wedged his broad shoulders between Kennedy's thighs and opened her to his intimate inspection. He trailed the tip of his middle finger down her slit, grinning when she bucked upward. Instead of sliding it inside her right away, he placed a row of kisses across her mound before lapping a path across her entire slit and back.

Only when she cursed and clutched the bedspread in one fist did he bury his face in her pussy and begin to eat her in earnest. Knox had to release his grip on his dick as her mewls of pleasure began to rain around them or he risked spraying her with his release before they'd barely gotten started.

Instead he returned his focus to her mouth, swallowing every sound of rapture she made as his hand romanced her chest, pinching, rubbing, and cupping. When he looked downward, Marcus had brought his hand up once again and was fitting his index and middle fingers to her opening.

Kennedy undulated beneath them, her body begging for more.

So they gave it to her. Marcus worked his digits within the tight, tight clutches of her pussy. He groaned as her heat and wetness surrounded him. His ass clenched as he rubbed his cock on the mattress and redoubled his efforts.

Knox tried not to be jealous but he wasn't nearly as good a person as Marcus or Kennedy. "Let me taste."

He imagined Marcus moving aside to give him access to her core. Instead, the other guy flashed Knox a wicked smile and dragged his fingers from within her. A wet noise that did nothing to calm Knox's dick accompanied the motion. Then he raised the glistening digits to Knox's mouth. He didn't know he'd find that unbelievably erotic until he was sliding his lips over Marcus's knuckles and sucking the arousal from his fingers.

Kennedy seemed to agree as she called out their names and shuddered beneath them.

Marcus withdrew his hand and slipped it back inside Kennedy, saying, "She's not going to last long. Why don't you push her over the top?"

Knox wasn't sure how exactly Marcus intended for him to do that until the guy practically smothered himself with Kennedy's pussy, gripped her hip with his free hand and rolled to his back, taking her with him. She was riding Marcus's face, leaving her ass completely exposed.

Marcus grabbed one of her ass cheeks and spread her wide, inviting Knox to rim her. He understood what was coming, where they were going, and couldn't wait to exceed even the wildest expectations Kennedy might have had for her first time. So he straddled Marcus to prep her, and if their cocks ground against each other while they pleasured her, well, that was a very happy accident.

Knox took over for Marcus, using his hands to spread Kennedy's ass wide, then touched the tip of his tongue to her hole. She squealed and bucked on Marcus's face but didn't tell them to stop. No, she cried out and shoved her backend higher in the air. Marcus raised up to keep contact with her pussy.

The sucking noises echoing from beneath him made Knox fairly sure Marcus was concentrating on Kennedy's clit. They weren't going to have a lot of time.

So he got to work. Knox groaned as he used his tongue to lap across the puckered ring of muscles at her entrance before swirling it around the outside and poking just the barest bit into it as she quivered beneath him. He licked as low as he could reach, his tongue flicking over Marcus's embedded finger for a second before returning to the center of her desire.

Kennedy's face was buried in the pillows, her shins and the fronts of her feet drumming on the bed as they drove her wild. Knox squeezed her ass then smacked it, causing her to cry out his name.

"You're going to come on his face, aren't you?" Knox asked her, wanting her to know that they couldn't wait to feel her flying apart between them. "Show him how much you love his mouth on you and maybe he'll give you more than a couple of fingers next."

Kennedy was incoherent as she clawed the bed. Marcus used his free hand to squeeze Knox's quad and he understood the message. Their girl was about to lose it.

So Knox pressed his pinky to her hole and licked around it, making sure it was plenty wet as he wedged it inside. She clamped down on him so hard he was afraid she might break him, but even if she did it would be worth it.

Knox wriggled his finger inside her as Marcus put his mouth to good use, and she screamed. It was very clearly a sound of ecstasy that shot straight to his dick, making it leak on Marcus's balls. He kept eating her ass as she came and came, threatening to drown Marcus as she did.

Only when her moans quieted to mewls and she went limp beneath him did Knox and Marcus show her mercy. They rolled her onto her side and rose so that they embraced her, Marcus kissing her softly before shocking Knox by lifting his face and swooping in for an aggressive lip lock of their own.

Kennedy hummed and reached for them both, rubbing the backs of their heads as they nipped at each other and wrestled for control. Knox let Marcus take the lead just so he could get some tiny measure of relief.

He had to fuck and it had to be soon.

Thankfully Kennedy didn't seem satisfied with a single orgasm, no matter how epic. "I'm ready, guys. I want you inside me. I want to know what it's like to fuck for real."

"Let me get some condoms." Marcus shifted as if to roll from the bed, but Kennedy refused to let him leave. She grabbed his cock and used her grip to keep him in place, making Knox laugh.

"That's my girl."

She beamed up at them and then said, "I've seen each of our medical records. There's no need for protection."

"And you use the ring." Marcus's lips tipped up at the corner. "I could feel it inside you."

"Does that mean what I think it means?" Knox didn't know how the day could get any better, but the thought of being inside his dream woman, bare, nearly made him shoot on the spot.

"It means hurry the hell up." A greedy Kennedy was a sexy Kennedy. "I'm tired of waiting."

"Yes, ma'am," Marcus teased, then looked to Knox. "Who's going first?"

12

Marcus called on every last scrap of patience he had while under the spell of Kennedy and Knox, both of whom were looking up at him as if waiting for him to make the call.

Kennedy chose for them. "Marcus."

She twined her fingers through Knox's, avoiding the appearance of favoritism. "Knox already had a turn."

"Fair enough." The other guy grinned, letting Marcus know there were no hard feelings. Besides, he *had* gotten to feel her sweet pussy wringing him the day before as she unraveled, and Marcus couldn't wait to do the same.

"And you can go after." Kennedy stretched between them. "Suddenly, I'm feeling especially needy."

"That's what happens when you finally let yourself free." Marcus cupped her cheek in his hand, adoring how she leaned her face into his touch. He couldn't believe he was going to have her after all this time. That she was going to accept him in return. So what if her ex was there with them too? Surprisingly, it didn't bother him. In fact, it helped him enjoy the moment more. He turned toward

Knox. "You'll tell me if I get carried away and push her too hard?"

"Yeah, man." Knox cradled Kennedy as she prepared to let Marcus in. She shifted and he tensed. "Here, let me scoot you over a bit."

Marcus realized she'd leaned on the worst of his injury by mistake. Kennedy must have surfaced enough to remember too. "How is it feeling? Do you need me to check your stitches?"

"Maybe much later, but I haven't done anything to mess them up...yet." Knox grinned. "And if I do, I know a doc who can put me back together again."

Kennedy frowned, some of her urgency receding.

"Seriously. It's fine. You make me feel so good I don't notice anything painful anymore." Knox kissed her tenderly. Marcus knew he was talking about far more than his physical wounds. He'd seen Knox's agony when he talked about his boyfriend and the shadows haunting his eyes when he'd explained how he'd gotten addicted to drugs.

Sex wasn't going to fix all that, but it was a mighty fine temporary distraction. They'd have to work on their issues and not just orgasms, though, or this would never last. Replacing drugs with the endorphin rush from fucking wasn't a viable long-term plan either. Not by itself, anyway.

"Stop looking at me like that. Both of you." Knox growled and reached around to smack Marcus's ass. "Don't let me kill the mood. Come on. Fuck."

Marcus would have to analyze later why Knox's command only served to turn him on more, but there was no denying his cock was ready and willing to get the job done.

"You're sure?" he asked Kennedy. She obviously didn't take sex lightly if she'd abstained all these years.

"If you don't get in there right now I'm going to scream." She clutched his shoulders, her trim nails digging miniature arcs into them, and wrenched.

Marcus couldn't believe he was there, in bed with her and her not-so-ex, about to join them together. That didn't stop him from doing as she directed. As Knox loosened her again with languid kisses and roaming hands, Marcus positioned himself between her legs. He held himself above the two lovers with a single straight-locked elbow, his hand planted beside their shoulders, then used his other hand to guide the fat head of his cock to her saturated opening.

The instant they connected, bare skin to skin, a flash of electricity went through him. This was a first for him too. He'd never been inside someone without a condom. It felt right to share this with her, and even Knox.

The other guy glanced down as Marcus began to feed her his dick, a bit at a time, in case she needed a moment to adapt. He shouldn't have worried. Kennedy hooked her legs in the small of his back and tried to force him deeper, faster.

"It's not a good idea to rush," he warned her. "Take a minute, get accustomed to having me inside you."

Fuck if that thought alone didn't make him grit his teeth to keep from coming before he'd even buried himself to the balls.

"If we went any slower, I'd be dead." Kennedy rolled her eyes and groaned when Marcus shifted within her. Knox was there, gliding his hand down her ribs then her belly to rub slow circles around her clit. She sighed and relaxed, allowing Marcus to slide in deeper. "Besides, I have toys way bigger than you."

Well, shit. That wasn't something he heard every day. He teased, "You know how to make a man feel special."

She laughed at that. Full-out laughed, with him wedged halfway into her.

"If you don't think he's remarkable, I don't stand a chance." Knox cracked up with them.

"I never said that." She melted right in front of them as Marcus settled within her. He withdrew, then drove forward with short strokes until he bottomed out. "Damn, I never had a vibrator that felt like that before."

Marcus grunted, because he'd never experienced a similar rush of sensations when fucking anyone before. She fit him perfectly, not only because of their matching desires, but because of the whole package—their beliefs, their emotions, and their pursuit of justice, in whatever form that took.

Kennedy understood him and she still wanted him.

Badly, if the hug of her pussy around his shaft was any indication.

"Damn, you feel so good on my cock." He caved to the urge to move, beginning to pump in and out of her with long, languid strokes.

"Feel amazing inside me," she murmured. When she reached down to fondle herself, Knox swept her hands away and did it for her. He cupped her breast in his left and then surprised Marcus by rotating so that he could lick her clit while Marcus fucked her.

That meant Knox's face rested on Marcus's abs. He used his free hand to pin the guy's head there, using it to bring Kennedy additional pleasure as he rode her.

"Oh!" Kennedy squirmed beneath Marcus, aligning

them so that the tip of his cock rubbed her in all the right places each time he plowed through her grasping channel of muscles to delight them both. "I'm close already. So full. So good."

Marcus was studying her so intently as he made love to her that he saw the instant she passed the point of no return. Her body strained toward him and Knox and the combined sensations they were imparting. He wanted to resist, to tag the other man to take up for him to stretch out his enjoyment, but at the same time, Marcus figured the benefit of having both of them there was that they could fully satisfy Kennedy by taking turns while allowing the other man to recover.

He had no doubt he'd recuperate quickly watching her and Knox go at it.

"Go ahead. I'm with you." Marcus stared straight into her eyes, willing her to trust him enough to finally let go. And she did.

Kennedy cried out, then became frantic, her body taking over and riding him as desperately as he was drilling into her. Knox followed her every motion, delivering unrelenting ecstasy as he sucked on her clit. She came around Marcus in a long, rolling orgasm that he never could have withstood.

He roared, then froze, as deep inside her as he could get. Come shot from his cock, flooding her with every drop he had in his balls. When the tidal wave of the first gush passed, his body took over on autopilot. He pounded into her at least a dozen more times as she milked him absolutely dry.

Knox made a strangled sound, then lifted off her right before Marcus collapsed, doing his best not to crush Kennedy as his heart pounded against hers. It had been every bit as good as he'd always known it would be, and what they'd done was only the start.

Marcus pulled out of her, a pearly trail stretching between them before decorating her pussy with the proof of what they'd experienced. Knox shocked him by leaning in and swallowing Marcus's softening cock at least halfway, which was pretty damn impressive. And when he drew off, he bent down and licked Kennedy clean.

Knox's raging hard-on told them as clearly as his blissed out expression, that he had enjoyed every second Marcus and Kennedy were joined.

"Go ahead." Marcus swapped places with the other man. "You've been waiting longer than me."

"I thought I'd ruined my chance at ever having this." Knox stared down at Kennedy, and for a moment, Marcus thought he might lose it entirely.

"Never stopped thinking about you." Kennedy hadn't entirely caught her breath. That didn't prevent her from reaching out and welcoming Knox between her legs. She hugged him as he fit himself to her and slid in considerably easier than Marcus had. Either because Marcus had stretched her open for the guy or because of the slick release he'd deposited within her.

Either way, Knox wasn't complaining.

Marcus snuggled up against Kennedy and tipped her face toward him so they could share a sweet kiss as Knox situated himself. When he'd embedded his dick fully within Kennedy, who groaned, he began to ride. Kennedy was stunning, and so responsive, it only took five or ten minutes of both men working over her to rekindle her passion.

Meanwhile, Knox was barely hanging on, fucking into her fast and hard while Marcus cushioned her against his momentum. Kennedy needed to catch up or Knox was going to come without her. And Marcus knew the other man wouldn't want that. Hell, Marcus wouldn't either. So he asked Kennedy, "How can I help you?"

"Tell me this means something to you." She surprised him by asking for an emotional connection that made her even more vulnerable than asking for a physical touch.

"Everything. It means *everything* to me," Marcus swore in between kisses. He cupped her breast in one hand, and Knox mimicked his motion on the other.

"And me." Knox's entire body had flushed. He was nearly vibrating with the strain of holding back.

"Then come in me. Don't hold back like you did yesterday. Don't leave me to feel this by myself and wonder if I'll ever be able to set you off too." Kennedy began to tense in Marcus's arms.

Knox made a strangled sound, then fell. He clutched her knees, on either side of him and threw his head back. His abdomen rippled before he pounded into Kennedy in a flurry of short, hard strokes that, along with Marcus's finger tapping her clit, set her off.

Kennedy screamed and came again, as Knox added to the mess inside her. His ass clenched then released as he shot jet after jet deep into her pussy. The base of his cock and balls turned frothy as he continued riding her through the crest of their passion.

And when it was over, he toppled onto the open side of the mattress, sucking in breaths that made the exertion of their workout at the gym look like a stroll in the park.

"Son of a bitch," Kennedy moaned, then covered her face with her hands. "What's wrong with me?"

Alarmed, Marcus and Knox sat up on either side of her. Marcus scanned over her, running a hand between her legs to make sure there wasn't any blood and that they hadn't used her too hard. Instead of flinching, she moaned.

"Still?" Marcus's eyes went wide and flew to Knox.

"Don't look at me. I'm gonna need a minute." Knox smiled wryly at them, then pried Kennedy's hands away so that he could exchange slow, sensual kisses with her.

"Me too." Marcus was more than willing even if his cock was taking a nap. "But I have an idea. I'll be right back."

"Where you going?" Knox shot him an exasperated glare.

"To raid her toy stash." He grinned.

"Oh, then hurry," Kennedy called out to him. "They're in the dresser beside my bed. The blue sparkly one is my favorite."

"Noted." Marcus sprinted across the hall buck-ass naked. He didn't give a single fuck if anyone watching on the security cameras saw. Most of the Shields and their Powertools, Hot Rods, and Hot Rides friends were kinky as fuck and would probably give him a thumbs-up anyway.

He used his retina and fingerprint to open her door, which she'd had programmed to permit him entrance and him the same for her, then dashed into her bedroom, both grateful and disappointed that he'd never realized what she had hidden in here when they'd been watching movies feet away.

He opened the top drawer and realized she hadn't been exaggerating. Holy fuck. The woman must own stock in rechargeable battery companies.

Grinning, he snagged the vibrator she'd indicated along with a little extra something they were definitely going to need. Because if fucking each of them separately hadn't fully satisfied her, they were going to have to up their game.

Marcus was so focused when he bolted from her apartment, letting the door slam, that he didn't notice Sola and Aarav having what looked like an argument in the hallway until Sola burst out laughing and reached for her cell phone to take a picture. She snorted. "Going good then?"

"Can't talk. Gotta go." Marcus waved in their direction. He realized he was waving the sparkly blue vibrator at them right about the time Sola's flash fired.

Ah fuck, she'd probably make that into the Shields' Christmas card or some shit.

It would be worth it.

Both she and Aarav were laughing when he disappeared into his apartment. At least he'd done something to help them even if it had meant exposing himself, literally. Once he got everything sorted out between him, Kennedy, and Knox, he was going to have a talk with Aarav. Because passing up the opportunity to have something he had known would be amazing was the stupidest thing he'd ever done. He didn't want that for his friends when they could have this instead.

Triumphant, he held the vibrator over his head as if it were some legendary sword instead of a sexual aide. Kennedy hummed while Knox fist pumped. Especially when he saw what else Marcus had brought with him. It was a very skinny wand vibrator with a curved tip and a definitely-not-full bottle of lube.

"You use this?" Knox asked. "In your ass?"

"Yep." Kennedy wasn't shy about it either. Marcus had to remind himself that she was a doctor. Bodies and their functions were her business, not anything she would shy away from. He felt himself falling for her even harder than before.

Knox looked to Marcus then back to the toy. "Are you thinking what I'm thinking?"

"I'm thinking you'd better take her ass. You're a lot thicker than that toy." Marcus tossed the other man the lube.

"And you...well... Yeah, you're right." Knox nodded.

"What am I missing here?" Kennedy raised a brow at both of them.

"We're going to get you off once with these." Knox paused to steal a quick kiss. "And after watching you enjoy yourself we'll be hard again and can show you how much better it is with us in their places."

"Exactly." Marcus held out his fist to Knox, who bumped it. He'd never imagined he'd be into sharing, but now he understood exactly why his friends loved group activities so much. He was able to give his partner so much more than he would have been able to manage on his own. "Assuming you still want more?"

"Now." Kennedy was on fire, so alive and openly sharing her desire that Marcus was almost afraid to look at her for fear of burning his eyes. She was incredible, even more amazing than he'd imagined.

They positioned her on her side with Marcus in front of her and Knox behind. Marcus took her knee in one hand and raised it, giving them room to work. Kennedy cupped her breasts as he fit the blue vibrator to her and slid it inside with a single stroke that stole her breath. Knox kissed the side of her neck, waiting for her to adjust before he lubed the small wand and then pressed it to her hole.

"Oh fuck," Kennedy hissed. "Never done them both at the same time before."

"Why not?" Marcus hoped he wasn't pushing her too hard. If she couldn't take the toys, she'd never be able to handle them.

"Not enough hands." Her tiny growl of frustration had him belting out a laugh.

Knox joined in before whispering to her, "Not a problem today."

Then he penetrated her with the narrow vibrator. They pumped them in and out of her slowly at first and gaining speed when her moans escalated too. And after a minute she said, "Turn them on. Not too high."

Marcus met Knox's stare over her, encouraged to see he was every bit as enflamed by what they were doing. In fact, his cock was already half-hard again, just like Marcus's, which was nudging Kennedy's thigh.

They worked together, doing as she asked in sync. The room was filled with a soft buzz and another sound he couldn't quite place. Kennedy's mouth worked but nothing came out.

"What is it?" Knox asked her as he stretched her ass open with the wand, pressing it in the spots that made Kennedy's eyes widen and her body quake.

"Push it in farther, Marcus." She showed him a bump on the side he hadn't quite noticed at first, and when he slid his finger over it, the small oval sucked at his finger.

"Ohhhh." He could see why this was her favorite. Marcus inserted the vibrator, which was doing some kind of squiggly dance, the middle moving in ways that would break his dick if he attempted it. And aligned the sucky spot with her clit.

Kennedy howled. She flung out her hands, one

grabbing him and the other latching onto Knox. She writhed between them. "I can't wait until this is your cocks fucking me."

"Sorry, no sucky bit on my dick," Marcus joked.

"It'll still be worth it," Kennedy panted. "But that thing turns me into an average guy, I swear. It can make me come in under a minute."

"Really?" He didn't doubt it based on how she was strung tight between him and Knox already.

"Yes. Gah." She was perspiring now, her skin dewy and rosy in the warm afternoon light. He'd never seen something more beautiful than her, surrendering to passion.

Knox groaned. "I hope you're ready for what you're doing to me."

Kennedy grinned and rocked back against him, driving the toy deeper and also brushing his reawakened cock with her ass. "That's not going to help me resist, you know?"

"Who told you to hold back?" Marcus leaned forward and bit her lip. "We want you to come. Want you to squeeze every last drop of pleasure you can from this moment."

"Oh. Damn." She grunted then unraveled, clawing at them as she climaxed again between them. Marcus could have watched her do that all day long. But this time when she opened her eyes, they were liquid with desire. They were making progress.

"You have one more in you," he told her as he extracted the vibrator from her and Knox did the same.

She couldn't speak, but she nodded before looking over her shoulder at Knox.

"Yeah. I'm good for it." He pumped his mostly stiff cock as Marcus did the same.

"Get your dick good and lubed," Marcus commanded.

Knox nodded, then slathered himself with the gel before tossing the container to Marcus. "Maybe you'd better do the same. I know she's soaked, and we...you know, but it's going to be a lot to handle."

"Good idea." Marcus looked to Kennedy and stroked the damp hair from her forehead. "Are you sure you're up for this? It's okay if you're worn out."

"I'm not about to waste a chance to have the two men I've always craved at the same time." Kennedy looked him dead in the eye. "Fuck me, Marcus."

Then she peered over her shoulder and growled, "You too. Fuck me."

Knox deferred to Marcus, as if waiting for him to devise a plan. So he said, "You get in there first. Get settled, and then I'll join you. You hold her and let me know if it's too much."

"It's never going to be enough," Kennedy murmured as if to herself.

Then Knox was doing as instructed, fitting himself to her ass and easing his way in. When her body relented and he sank in an inch or two in one go, Knox grunted. Kennedy gasped and held her breath. Knox froze and Marcus swooped in, kissing Kennedy to distract her until the initial twinge of discomfort dissipated.

After a minute or two, she broke away and angled her face so Knox could have a taste. When he did, she murmured, "I'm okay now. Keep going."

He proceeded slowly, drilling deeper gradually until she held all of him. Only then did he pause, wrapping his arms around her and giving Marcus the green light.

Marcus draped her top leg over Knox's, then scooted closer, sandwiching her between them. He aimed his cock at her pussy, groaning when it slipped out of place and tapped Knox's shaft instead. They both cursed.

"Sorry." Marcus didn't know what etiquette dictated in this circumstance, but when his gaze clashed with Knox's it certainly wasn't disgust that he observed.

"I'm not." Knox bit Kennedy's shoulder hard enough to leave a mark, but she only moaned and opened her legs wider.

So Marcus got back to business, sliding around until he notched the head of his cock in her opening and then advanced. She was tighter, making it slower going than the first time he'd been inside her but even more glorious knowing that he and Knox were fulfilling all of her fantasies and about to fuck her until she was boneless with rapture.

There was no way he could have satisfied her by himself. Knowing that, he was glad they'd waited until Knox came back into her life to share this experience. Thankful that chance had brought them all together at exactly the perfect moment even if he'd cursed how long it had taken before he'd realized what was needed to do this right.

In a sense, she'd admitted to him that she needed Knox. He just hadn't understood that was a possibility, and neither—he believed—had she. But watching her face as Knox plowed her ass with long, slow strokes that Marcus moved in counterpoint to, he knew it was what she'd always desired.

Overwhelmed with gratitude and pure blazing rapture, Marcus leaned across Kennedy and captured Knox's mouth with his own. The kiss they shared was artless and raw as they concentrated on keeping their strokes within Kennedy steady and languid. Their cocks rubbed against each other, only a thin bit of her body separating them.

And *that* seemed to finally be enough for Kennedy.

She clamped down on them both, clutching them within her, hugging them with her body as she shattered around them. She clawed at Marcus's back and squeezed Knox's flank, holding them tight against her as she spiraled into a powerful and long-lasting orgasm.

Neither man had the power to resist her reaction. They fell with her, coming, rocking until they were spent and melted into a pile of cuddles and kisses.

None of them ruined the moment by talking or putting even a millimeter of distance between them. Instead they wound down together with a series of soft touches, easy kisses, and sighs.

Before long, Knox and Kennedy's breathing became the measured inhalations that only accompanied slumber.

While Marcus's body might have been exhausted, his mind was not ready to disengage. So he lay there the entire afternoon, watching Knox and Kennedy snuggle in his arms, wondering when they were going to realize that they didn't need him to chaperone them and kick him out of his own bed.

Somehow that thought wrecked him even worse than it would have when he only cared about Kennedy. Because now Marcus understood why she'd been so hung up on Knox, and thought it would be easy for him to fall under the other guy's spell if he wasn't careful.

That was dangerous business. Until this operation ended, they were in jeopardy of being manipulated. Of being played. He had to remember where Knox came from and what his old buddies would be willing to do to either get him back or make sure he was never a problem for them again.

Otherwise all three of them were going to pay the price.

<h1 style="text-align:center">13</h1>

Kennedy tried to tone down the shit-eating grin she'd been sporting since waking up between Marcus and Knox and found out that what she'd thought was the best dream she'd ever had was actually reality. *Damn.*

As if having Knox back in her life, and hopefully ready to implement some positive changes in his own, wasn't miracle enough, seeing him and Marcus get along—and make out while fucking her—had absolutely blown her mind. There had to be less of a chance of that happening than a woman being diagnosed with agammaglobulinemia. And now here they were, hanging out in the communal dining hall on the ground floor of the Shields' headquarters.

It was a wide-open space with a state-of-the-art stainless everything kitchen along one wall. A long butcher block table with comfy padded leather benches stretched along the other. James had custom built the furniture and all the cabinetry, which was painted a dusty blue. He'd covered the walls with a subtly iridescent subway tile that looked like freshly fallen snow in the moonlight. Nolan's girlfriend, Laurel, and one of the Powertools wives, Kate, who owned an antique restoration and decorating business, had decorated the space with plenty of plants and contemporary farmhouse flair to lend it a homey rather than an institutional feel.

It had become a tradition for them to eat together, Shields and significant others and occasionally their Middletown friends from the Powertools, Hot Rods, or Hot Rides, too. On that night, some of them cooked, a few split a pizza, and the rest brought their own previously prepared meals from their apartments upstairs. It wasn't a requirement to join in, but their careers could be isolating. Spending time with people who got it, and shared common goals, was as nourishing for their souls as their food was for their bodies.

"Wow. It's awesome that you have so many people to watch your back," Knox leaned toward Kennedy and murmured to her.

"They're more than simply co-workers. They're my friends. A support system." Kennedy glanced over at Sola, who winked at her. Ruby flashed her a thumbs-up. She couldn't wait to talk privately with the women since they'd obviously caught on to the vibe between her, Marcus, and Knox immediately.

"Since you were too *busy* to answer our damn texts earlier, we ordered your usuals," Sola said to Marcus and Kennedy before turning to Knox. "Sorry, we weren't sure what you liked. There's plenty of pizza. Help yourself."

"You want some of my sausage sandwich?" Marcus asked politely as he unwrapped it.

Every single Shield in the room cracked up before

Liam busted their balls. "I thought you were saving your sausage for Kennedy, homie."

"Nah. I prefer the meat*ball* sub, thanks." Kennedy bit into it with relish, making the men in the room groan. Aarav covered his crotch with one hand, inspiring Sola and Ruby to laugh twice as hard.

Knox looked between Marcus and Kennedy. She wasn't sure if he would play along or bolt until he grinned. "Maybe I'll have a little of both. Anyone got a taco to go with it? I'm a fan of variety."

When Kennedy blushed and Marcus only chuckled knowingly, everyone else grew quiet. James slapped his hands on the table, his eyes huge. Tact was not his forte. "Wait. Did you guys *finally* do it? And with him, too?"

In their close-knit team, privacy wasn't a thing. Hell, almost everyone in the room—Nolan's and James's significant others excluded—had already seen and heard her fuck Knox. *Oops.*

"You're just now figuring that out?" Sola teased him. "Haven't you seen the way they're clinging to our girl and how damn happy yet exhausted she looks. Come on, you've had enough group sex to know what all that adds up to."

"You're right. I have." James buffed his perfectly manicured nails on his Robin T-shirt before his wife, Devon, teasingly smacked his shoulder.

Kennedy didn't confirm or deny. She did, however, keep right on smirking and licked sauce from her fingertips deliberately, not-so-secretly relishing the attention both men paid to her every tiny move.

"Well, damn," Ruby joked. "I guess I'm going to have to find myself a couple of studs to try out this threesome shit with since you all seem to recommend it so highly."

Ace raised his unbroken arm, probably because he was on a pretty hefty dose of pain pills. Kennedy had instructed him to make sure they stayed locked up in his and Liam's place so they couldn't be any sort of temptation for Knox. "Liam and I got you covered."

Liam shot Ace a glare and yanked on his wrist until he lowered his hand. "Quit it."

"Probably best not to fuck where I work." Ruby looked to Sevan—Ransom and Levi's wife—who was smothering an amused expression with her napkin. "How about the Hot Rides or the Hot Rods? They have any unattached sexy mechanic friends?"

"Unfortunately, they're taken and living the settled life these days." Sevan rested her head on Levi's shoulder while Ransom rubbed a slow circle on her lower back.

"Damn. I guess I'll keep repping for Team Single then." Ruby flipped a crimson lock over her shoulder.

"Me too," Aarav grumbled, and kicked out a corner of one of the benches so he could swing into a spot across from Sola, who concentrated a little too hard on her own meal. "Relationships are too damn much work."

Kennedy stared at the guy. He was handsome, his thick, defined brows slashing across his tanned skin, which highlighted rich brown eyes that often observed every detail of his surroundings. He was calm and usually so outwardly neutral that they'd referred to him as a machine, especially when he was behind his sniper rifle. Lately, though, like now, he seemed a bit frustrated. She wondered what the hell was keeping him from approaching Sola as everyone but her best friend knew he wanted to do.

"Well, if you change your mind, we live right across

the hall from you," Ace kept rambling at Ruby despite Liam's obvious shut-the-fuck-up glare.

"Yes, I'm well aware." She didn't seem to mind. "You're not the quietest neighbors I've ever had, you know."

"Oh. Oops." Ace didn't seem very sorry.

Liam, on the other hand, choked on one of the healthy grilled chicken salads he'd assembled for him and Ace. Kennedy made a mental note to ask Ruby exactly what she'd heard through the walls. Interesting.

"Speaking of relationships, I, uh, was wondering what you all thought about us maybe holding a reception. Here, at Shields." Sevan looked around the room as if waiting for someone to say it was a stupid idea. It was only recently that she'd discovered this found family and become part of it like Kennedy had too. "I know we upset some people—ahem, my sister mostly—when we eloped. So..."

"That's the best idea I've heard in a while." James clapped and pulled out his infamous planner from beneath the table. He started flipping pages and extracted an entire rainbow's worth of colored pens from a pouch in the back. "When are you thinking? Maybe in June. That will give us time to talk to a florist, and taste-test catering, and arrange for a photographer, and—"

"I promised you wouldn't have to worry about a thing, didn't I?" Levi laughed when Sevan hopped up and jogged over to James.

"Bless you." She hugged him. "That's one reason we slipped away to get it over with. Planning and everyone watching me after years of fading into the shadows. It was overwhelming. But I see now that we hurt Joy by not including her, which was never my intent. Can you help me make it right?"

"Oh, honey, let's bring Joy in on this. We'll put her in charge of a bunch of stuff. Together we'll figure out your vision. Then I'll create an inspiration board, and once we have your style nailed down, I'll buddy up with Joy and we'll arrange everything. The only thing you'll have to do is show up and have a magical night with those two hunks of yours while your sister preens and shows everyone how proud of you and happy for you she is. It will be a kick ass party and stress-free for you, I swear." James gave her a loud, smacking kiss on her cheek.

"Thanks." Sevan turned away and knuckled something from the corner of her eye. She'd grown up alone, then hidden in plain sight pretending to be a young man in order to take down the president of a motorcycle club. Being able to rely on people who knew and loved her for her true self was still new and kind of scary, Kennedy assumed.

Before they could get too far into the details, Jordan strode into the dining hall. He didn't have his husband, music legend Kason Cox, or his wife, Wren, a welder who worked at Hot Rides, with him. That was unusual, unless...his popping in had more to do with work than pleasure.

Sure enough, a couple of strangers followed close behind him. Both, all business. The taller of the two had close-cropped dark hair with an especially neat beard that was offset by his partner's shaggy reddish facial hair and messy topknot.

"You hungry?" Liam held the open pizza box toward their boss, who snagged a slice of pepperoni.

"Sorry to interrupt dinner." Jordan leaned against the counter and bit off damn near half of the piece of pizza at once. Had he not even taken time to eat that day yet?

When Liam swung the leftovers toward the newcomers, both shook their head no in unison.

"Since Ace is going to be sitting on the sidelines for a while and some of us have family with us here..." Jordan motioned toward Nolan, who was perched between his girlfriend, Laurel, and his boyfriend, Jace. "I figured we could use a few extra set of eyes around at least until we've figured out this situation with Knox and the Vipers."

"Never hurts." Marcus took a deep breath, as if he'd been worried too.

"Everybody, this is Legend." Jordan pointed to the man who seemed like he could have been part black bear given his size and the thick, dark fur that coated his arms and peeked from the three open buttons at the top of his light gray, ribbed shirt. "And that's Tavish. Don't ask where they came from because they can't tell you. Know that they were highly recommended by people I trust and I'm happy to have them onboard, especially right now."

Knox blew out a breath and scrubbed his hands over his face. "I'm sorry to be bringing shit to your door."

"You haven't yet," Jordan pointed out. "I'd rather be over prepared in case trouble finds us. Either way, we're glad to have you so that we have a shot at shutting some of this down for good."

When Kennedy looked around the room, she saw respect in her fellow Shields' gazes, which wasn't always easy to earn.

Knox swallowed hard and nodded. "I'll do whatever I can to help."

"Let's move this party into the command center." Jordan jerked his head in that direction.

"Damn it. I'm starving," Nolan grumbled as he eyed

his pizza as if debating whether to stuff the remainder in his mouth at once.

"Bring your dinner with you. Just move." Jordan pointed.

"You trust him with red sauce on our new carpet?" James seemed horrified.

"Absolutely not. How's this? Bring your dinner and don't spill any or James will dock your pay to clean the carpet." Jordan grinned, knowing full well they made enough to buy a whole new one for every meeting if necessary.

"Worth it." Nolan swiped a napkin over his mouth, then swooped in to kiss first Laurel and then Jace, both of whom were laughing. He lowered his voice then. "If this goes late, don't wait up. At least I'll have thoughts of what the two of you are doing in bed to keep me occupied."

"Or...you could concentrate so you don't get someone killed by being a horndog." Sola flicked a garlic knot at Nolan.

He caught it and popped the whole thing into his mouth before mumbling around it, "I'm great at multitasking."

"I can attest to that." Laurel wiggled her brows, giggling.

But as she and the rest of the family members huddled up and the Shields filed out into the boardroom, the atmosphere in the room chilled considerably. Unfortunately, Kennedy didn't think it had anything to do with the state-of-the-art HVAC system James and the Powertools had installed for them.

14

They filed into the command center, Ruby taking her station at the computer brains for the audiovisual equipment, Jordan at the head of the table, and the rest of them scattered around. As easy as things had been in the dining room, they were nearly as tense then as when Kennedy was working on someone in the field.

Knox cleared his throat and spoke up. "What can I tell you?"

Jordan planted his elbows on the table, steepled his fingers, and leaned in. "Start talking, and as you hit on something that sounds interesting, I'll figure out what I want to know more about."

"Sure." Knox took a deep, ragged breath. "I got involved with the Vipers when I was seventeen. I was recruited by the local cops when I expressed an interest in joining the force after graduation. They told me I'd almost surely get a spot in the academy if I could prove myself first by being a mole."

"Son of a bitch." Aarav clenched his jaw. "They didn't look after you, did they?"

Knox shrugged. "I had to fit in to get any good dirt. That meant rolling with them when they smoked. Unfortunately, I apparently inherited my mom's love of drugs."

He stared at a spot directly in front of him, so Kennedy reached over beneath the table and squeezed his thigh. She was surprised when she did, that her knuckles brushed against Marcus's as he did the same on Knox's other leg.

"And the cops didn't offer to help you?" Jordan cursed. "This is why so many of us left. Why we have our own code of what's right and wrong. I'm sorry they used you like that."

Knox nodded tersely, as if he might crack if he spoke his thanks aloud. He chewed his nails and Jordan didn't press him, letting him inhale a few shaky breaths before proceeding. He glanced around the room, as if searching for the exit, until his gaze landed on Nolan's throat flexing as he sipped from a silver can.

"Is that a beer?" Knox eyed it as if it were made of diamonds instead of hops and water.

"Uh, yeah. You know what? Shouldn't have it at a work meeting anyway." Nolan stepped into the bathroom and poured it down the sink without a second thought.

Knox sighed and resumed mauling his poor abused fingernails with his teeth.

The immensity of what they were asking him to do smacked Kennedy in the face. Could Knox handle the pressure? Would he crack and return to his old ways? Struggling with sobriety was hard enough. All this extra shit on top could send him spiraling into darkness again.

Now that she'd found him again, she couldn't stand the thought of him being lost.

"Okay, so, anyway. Recently, the stakes have been higher. Those of us who oversaw large regions started getting shipments of special shit. We were told to charge double for it and only give it to our best customers. Problem was, it was too good. A lot of people, my ex and I included, couldn't handle it. We both OD'd." Knox swallowed and looked at the bathroom as if considering lapping the beer out of the sink. "For some reason, paramedics brought me back."

He snatched his stare from the bathroom and instead looked at Kennedy. Was she really ready to be his purpose? Was Marcus?

"What happened to your girlfriend?" Jordan wondered.

"Boyfriend. He died."

"Shit. I'm so sorry, man," James said softly as the rest of the Shields added their condolences.

"So yeah, that sucked." Understatement of the century. "It might also be important to know his name was Riggs, and he was Vex's nephew."

"Vex as in the head of the Vipers." Jordan confirmed.

"Yeah."

"So you have some special connection to the guy." Jordan tapped his fingers on the table at that.

"Not really. I think he trusted me more because of it, though. Because he knew from Riggs that I was all in… until I wasn't. Riggs cared more about advancing than I did and I went along with a lot of the plans Vex had for us because it kept things flowing. Once Riggs died, though, the memories from that night kept me clean and I lost the will to be involved. I didn't touch one fucking bit of that shit you saw in the cabin the other day. It's no joke. It's going to kill a lot of people if it hits the streets."

"What is it?" Jordan asked.

"All I know is our boss told us it's a test. Only two places had the recipe and they weren't fucking around, keeping a tight lid on it, so they can hopefully smash the competition once and for all." Knox pinched the bridge of his nose. "That's why I ratted to that shitty agent when I found out one of the locations where they were cooking it."

"They intercepted the delivery you informed them about and were able to shut down the plant. But they haven't been able to locate the source of the remaining supply." Jordan must have known at least some of what Knox was sharing. He'd used it to confirm Knox was being straight with them.

As much as Kennedy hated to admit it, she appreciated that. A sliver of her was still afraid to fully put her faith in him given how fragile his recent commitment to doing the right thing might be in the face of his addiction issues. He'd wrecked her once. If he didn't live up to the high hopes she was already forming, it would destroy her this time around.

And now it wasn't only her in the equation. She had to worry about the fallout harming Marcus too. Hell, even their professions were at risk. Her whole life.

"Okay, I have a question." Ruby raised her hand from the computer console like the geek-at-heart she was. Liam and Ace exchanged an amused glance.

"Yeah?" Knox raised his gaze to hers.

"How did you communicate with the people who worked for you and especially with this Vex dude?" She twirled a section of her red hair around her finger.

Knox rattled off the name of a communication app. "You want my phone?"

"Uh huh." Ruby nodded. He unlocked it then tossed it to her. She snagged it with one hand, then beamed. "I've got this. Continue."

She flipped around and started hammering on the keyboard, completely ignoring everything they were saying. JRad, her mentor from the Men in Blue, had a hell of a reputation in their industry, but Kennedy had no doubt the student would surpass the teacher someday, if she hadn't already.

"Unfortunately, that's pretty much what I know. They were keeping us in the dark about most of the operation. I got the feeling they were on the cusp of making this shit able to be mass produced instead of putting out small test batches." Knox shrugged.

"Okay, let me make a few calls and then we can pick up again." Jordan snagged the headset James held out to him, then ducked behind the display screens into the nook where Kennedy had kissed Marcus during the grand opening.

When she glanced over at him, he was grinning back, obviously reliving the same memory.

"I'm sorry I'm such a fucking loser." Knox ripped a bit of skin from his cuticle, making Kennedy wince. She took his hand in hers and lifted it to her mouth, kissing the raw spot he had aggravated.

"You're not." Marcus angled his chair to face Knox squarely.

James joined them, hopping up so that he sat on the table beside Kennedy. He swung his legs, his hot pink sneakers zipping through the air. "Hey, I thought I'd come over and say I really admire you for doing this. I know it's hard enough to open up about your personal life, but doing it in front of these do-gooders must be extra difficult."

Kennedy silently thanked James for easing the tension. Of course he was an exceptional communicator having been part of a committed threesome and also having six additional lovers as part of the Powertools crew. If they weren't open and honest, their complex lifestyle would never work.

"Uh, thanks. I guess." Knox groaned. "Don't make me out to be some kind of hero, though. I'm just a junkie who ruined his chances with a woman way too good for him."

"From my perspective, your odds with that lady look pretty damn stellar," James said with a kind smile. "And maybe even for a two-fer with an equally great guy. This pair should have been a perfect match on their own, yet somehow never quite got things to work between them until you showed up. Just saying."

Knox lifted his head then and looked between Marcus and Kennedy. "Yeah, why is that exactly?"

"Because sometimes people need a third person to bring them together. Or keep them together. My wife, Devon, did that for Neil and me. We probably wouldn't have lasted without her." James shook his head as if chasing that horrible possibility from his mind.

Aarav ambled closer, taking up a spot beside Marcus though he looked at James, not Knox when he asked, "Could you say more about that?"

Kennedy tried to play it cool, but her heart was thundering. Could he be asking for himself? Was there some reason he thought having another person around might make it easier for him to approach Sola?

Her best friend was across the room, joking around

with Nolan and Liam. Aarav couldn't seem to go more than three seconds without glancing over his shoulder at her to make sure she was still there and safe although there was no threat to them in the office, despite the thunder that had begun rumbling in the distance. The news had predicted strong storms that evening and it looked like they had been right.

"I guess Neil and I were kind of stubborn. Stuck in our way of doing things. Which was okay for a while, but Devon brought out parts of us that we held in check around each other. She lets me be silly and goof around with her, and she lets Neil explore the side of him that gets off with women. As for her, she likes to take the lead with me but surrender to him. It's just different than how we are alone. And without her...we might not have been enough for each other. Neil and I had started arguing a lot even though I knew he was my person. We couldn't seem to get it together until Devon whipped us into shape."

Aarav slicked back his wavy obsidian hair with his palm. "I know that feeling."

"Can I give you some unsolicited and probably shitty advice?" Knox asked.

"Sure." Aarav grinned. "Can't be any worse than I'm doing myself. Hell, you've been here like two days and you've already snagged a couple of amazing people."

"Uh, yeah. I guess. Though I'm pretty sure they *snagged* me." Knox finally cracked the hint of a smile. "Anyway, if we're talking about that firecracker of a brunette over there, you should probably quit thinking so hard and do something. She keeps looking over at you like she'd rather have you than that pizza for dinner."

"She does?" Aarav peeked over his shoulder at the

same time Sola looked their way, as if she could feel the heat of his stare.

"Yes," Marcus, Kennedy, Knox, and James all said at exactly the same moment.

"She's waiting for you to make a move." Marcus elbowed Aarav. "How many times have I told you this?"

"Sola isn't the kind of woman to sit back. If she liked me, she'd have said so by now." Aarav's shoulders slumped. "That's one of the things I appreciate about her. She knows what she wants and she goes and gets it."

"Maybe not when it comes to love." James leaned in. "None of us think straight when our hearts are involved. The consequences of a wrong decision are too fucking scary. So...Knox..."

"Huh?" Knox looked up at James then. "Welcome to Shields. Don't make me have to sic my wife on you. She will not hesitate to kick your ass if you mess with our friends, okay?"

Knox laughed at that. Kennedy squeezed James tight and whispered, "Thank you."

"I never meant to let you down," Knox promised Kennedy. "And I'll do my best to make sure it doesn't happen again." This time he also looked at Marcus, who nodded.

As if the universe heard and punctuated the oath, a blinding light flashed through the entire command center followed immediately by a blast of thunder that had all of them rocketing to their feet and staring out the tinted glass at the back parking lot.

They were just in time to see a glorious oak tree that had withstood who knew how many storms crack straight down the center. Half remained standing while the rest teetered and then tipped, picking up steam as it crashed straight toward the corner of the lot where James parked his neon-green itty-bitty hybrid car to keep it away from people like Nolan, who had backed into it most recently.

"Noooooooooooooooooooooooo!" James sprinted toward the glass and threw his palms up on it as the tree belly-flopped onto the roof, leaving a giant crater.

For a moment, there was dead silence. Then the entire command center broke out into a roar of laughter. Kennedy put her hands on her cheeks both in shock and to keep her face from splitting as she cracked up. Marcus clutched his gut and several of the men hooted.

"What the hell is wrong with all of you?" Knox jogged over to James. "Was that your car? Oh my God, dude. I'm sorry."

Tears streamed down Kennedy's face as everyone only cackled harder. Everyone but Ruby, who was lost in her ones and zeros. In their line of work there had to be a way to destress, and this...this was priceless.

Marcus was already hauling his phone from his pocket and tapping his contacts. "Hey, Roman? You're never going to guess what just happened."

He paused to catch his breath although a snort escaped.

"James's car got squashed by a tree. Can you come tow it to the shop and fix it up again?" Kennedy heard the other man curse a streak from the other end of the line. "Dead serious. Send Bryce with the flatbed. I know, I know, that thing has spent more time at your garage than out of it. Thanks, man. And...while you're here, there's someone I'd like you to meet. Maybe you can talk to him about some shit he's going through?"

Kennedy beamed at Marcus. He was such a good man. Of course he'd want to help Knox through his addiction issues. Roman had struggled himself. He would know better than them how to help Knox navigate the tough times ahead. Knox was trying, but was it for their sake, or his own?

Either way, she was glad for Marcus's and Roman's support.

"What the hell are you all..." Jordan rejoined them, his headset in his hand. When he looked out the window, he didn't bust a gut, but he wasn't able to suppress his smirk either. "Well, isn't that something."

James flipped them all off with a double bird, then sulked as he plopped into one of the fancy chairs he'd ordered for the command center. He might have cursed them out if Ruby hadn't jumped up right then.

"Got it!" She pumped her fist and blinked, as if only then noticing their insanity. She peeked out the window, then chuckled before returning her gaze to Jordan. "We don't have a lot of time."

Jordan took his seat again at that. "What'd you find?"

"The Vipers are sending a pair of drivers to pick up a shipment from two 'factory workers.'" She used air quotes. "They're making it a small op to avoid drawing attention from authorities or the people who gunned down the guys they sent to reclaim Knox and their previous cache. By the way, they think that he's gone rogue and started his own operation with that last batch, so they're not really onto us...yet."

Jordan thought about that for a minute, then sat back in his chair, staring at Knox. "I think you're going to get that chance you wanted to prove yourself."

Oh fuck no. Kennedy was sure that whatever came out of her boss's mouth next, she was going to hate it. And she was right.

"What are you thinking?" Knox wondered, not saying no.

"You're going to pick up that delivery for us. And if you can't also figure out where they're sending it from, you'll bring the drivers back to us, so we can find out for you." Jordan didn't say it in so many words, but Kennedy knew what he meant. Someone on their team would torture the men if they needed to, and in any case, they wouldn't be leaving Shields headquarters alive.

"Me? Don't you think they're going to have a head's up that I'm not on the old boss's Christmas card list anymore?" Knox asked.

"Do you think they'll care that much if you show up with twice as much money as they're expecting plus an offer of a fuck ton more in exchange for the recipe?" Jordan lifted one shoulder.

"They're not idiots. They know what real cash looks like." Knox waved his hands in front of his chest.

"We've got ten million in our safe in the basement and I can get more if we need it." Jordan wasn't fucking kidding either. James had paid special attention to the facilities down there. No one could get in, or out, of that part of the building without help from the team. It was where they stashed valuables, either currency or bad guys, until they were done with them.

"Oh. Well. Then yeah. I guess that'll work." Knox refused to look at Marcus or Kennedy.

Was it because he knew she'd be freaking out about him putting himself in danger like that, or because he didn't want them to see that he intended to double cross them when he had his hands on either the money or the drugs?

The fact that the thought crossed her mind, even for

an instant, meant they still had a long way to go before they could ever have a relationship that lasted beyond an afternoon of endless orgasms.

But would they get the chance to work on it, or would he be taken from her again before they'd hardly had a chance to find out?

15

Knox had no doubt this was going to be one of the worst nights of his life. Now that he'd found something worth hanging around for, the stakes had skyrocketed. Whereas before, he hadn't really given a shit about what happened to him, now he had two compelling reasons to keep his hide free of more bullet holes.

Then again, maybe all he was doing was putting Marcus and Kennedy in danger. He might never be able to escape his past or outrun the Vipers. He'd keep bringing this bullshit to their front door over and over unless he did something to change that.

So there he was, driving a box truck full of legit hundred dollar bills toward the rendezvous point the Vipers had been supposed to approach. Meanwhile, Nolan had been deployed to make sure the original couriers never arrived. How exactly he was going to manage that hadn't been explained to Knox, but he was pretty sure it involved some of the assholes he used to work with becoming unalive.

Knox focused on his role in this mission. He had one task: get the delivery crew to trust him enough that they handed over the drugs and any information they had on the location of the recipe. And if he couldn't get that out of them, help Marcus and the Shields get them into custody so they could do more investigating while he took their stash off the streets.

Again.

If he wasn't good for anything else, he considered that his new personal undertaking. Keeping some stupid seventeen-year-old out there from wrecking their life, like he had his own.

If he managed to make it back to Kennedy, and proved to her that he deserved her trust when it came to sharing more than just her body, well...that was almost too much to hope for when he likely wasn't going to survive this encounter.

Knox looked over to Marcus and said, "Last chance. You want out?"

"Fuck off." Marcus didn't even bother to meet his gaze.

"You really do shit like this all the time?" Knox shook his head. "Maybe you're dumber than I am."

"Maybe I have a low tolerance for injustice." Marcus shrugged as if it was no big deal that he was so damn *good*.

"We're almost there." Knox glanced at the GPS and the route James had programmed remotely for him.

Marcus grunted and sat so still Knox knew he was looking in every direction at once. They rolled through a dilapidated chain link fence and into a parking lot behind an abandoned factory. He parked in the spot immediately next to an identical unmarked white vehicle. Knox slid from the driver's seat, hoping that the Shields were the only people lurking out in the shadows beyond the ring of patchy illumination tossed onto the cracked pavement by the flickering florescent lights above.

"What the fuck?" the driver of the other truck said as he drew his gun. "You're not Dino."

"No shit." Knox shrugged. "You know who I am, though?"

"The guy who bailed on the Vipers. Why the fuck shouldn't I blow your head off and send your body back to Vex for a bonus?"

"I've got about six million reasons right here." Knox rolled up the back door of the box truck and let them see the cash piled inside. He hoped they didn't look too closely at a couple of the crates in the corners where Sola and Liam were hidden.

"There's a new boss in town." Marcus crossed his arms and angled his head so his diamond studs flashed in the overhead light. He impressed the hell out of Knox, and apparently the manufacturers too.

The two guys looked at each other and then back to Knox, who shrugged. "Let's be honest, you're smart enough to understand that if we're here instead of the Vipers, we've already secured the distribution end of this supply chain. No reason why we couldn't make you two obsolete and keep the delivery if we want. So you might as well do the smart thing and take what we're offering. There's more to come if we partner long-term on this new project."

There was a long pause and then the taller of the two delivery guys shrugged. "Yeah. Okay. As long as you're going to keep selling what we're making. Not only for this one shipment. And we need to check the cash."

"That's the idea. Go grab some at random to verify. But there isn't time to go through it all." Knox thought of their teammate cargo, more precious than money. James had promised the crates were lined with bulletproof panels, but it still made him nervous to have Sola and Liam bundled up like sitting ducks back there. "Besides, how do we know your haul is as quality as people are saying? I guess we'll both have to take it on faith."

"Nah. You're about to sample some while we look at the money. No one's gonna come back on us saying it's bullshit stuff." The driver planted his feet.

Knox's heart rate spiked and he nearly stumbled backward, but he bumped into Marcus. He knew then they weren't getting out of there without one of them testing the drugs. That's how they always did things during these major transactions. And no way in fucking hell was he going to let Marcus touch that shit.

Over the comms, Kennedy shrieked. He desperately tried to block out her sobs, begging him not to do what needed to be done. When he glanced back at Marcus, he saw a million different things in the other man's eyes, but in the split second they had it would have been impossible to formulate any sort of alternate plan. In the world Knox was from, taste testing wasn't a big deal. If they didn't do it, they were both likely to end up killed.

So Knox agreed. "Yeah, give me some."

"I have them in my sights. I can take them out instead. Say the word." Aarav had set up sniper shop on some nearby building.

"Hold." Jordan's voice rang through. "We need them alive to find out the location of the factory and info on the recipe. Unless Marcus can get it out of them right now, we'll have to move forward."

Marcus cleared his throat. "We'll take your word for it

if you can tell us more about where it's being made or what's in that shit."

"Nah, man. We ain't dumb. You already trashed a bunch of Vipers, why not us next? What we know about that is the only thing making us useful." The guy shook his head, glancing over his shoulder as he rummaged through the wads of cash, apparently satisfied with what he saw. "One of you hit that shit, then let's get the fuck out of here before someone else makes a better offer or decides to be less civilized about it, eh?"

"Son of a bitch," James hissed.

There was no other option. Knox nodded and stepped forward. He waited for the passenger to unlock their van and withdraw a brick at random. Knox took out his knife, flipped it open, and sliced a line in the plastic wrapping. He dipped just the tip of his blade in the white substance and dropped the granules onto the truck bed, where he smashed them with the handle of his switchblade hard enough to make the delivery guy flinch.

Knox stared at Marcus, bent down, and snorted the drugs off the metal bed.

Immediately, he was reliving that night. The worst night of his life before this one. Chemicals flew straight to his brain and started buzzing around like a swarm of flies on a dead body. Maybe it was his corpse they were hovering over. He had only done a tiny bit, thought it was a small enough hit that it wouldn't be a danger like it had been last time when he'd been overconfident, but then again, he hadn't had anything in his system for damn near three months.

"It's gooood." Fuck, was he already slurring? It wasn't a lie either. His heart started beating triple time and he swore he developed night vision.

"Time to go," Jordan instructed in their ears. "Now, Marcus, so you can get Knox to help as soon as possible."

"We'll take it." Marcus held out his hand and shook with the driver of the other van. It was the break they needed to have the slight advantage required in order to take the delivery guys alive. If only it had come a moment earlier, if the scales had tipped in their favor sooner, maybe the evening could have ended before Knox had sacrificed himself.

As it was, it was going to be dicey.

Marcus used the connection of his hand, clasped in the delivery guy's, as leverage. He swung the bastard's smug expression into the corner of the truck. His co-pilot had a gun and whipped it up, aimed at Marcus. Without hesitation, Knox threw himself at the fucker. The problem was, the drugs flooded his veins with fire and overconfidence so he only clipped the asshole instead of tackling him.

It was about then that roars echoed around them. Liam and Sola flew over Knox as they bolted from the back of the money truck and made quick work of disarming and suppressing the second delivery guy. Before Knox could manage to find his feet in the distorted world, they'd captured and bound the two drug traffickers, did something to make them go quiet and still, then locked them in the back of the truck with the money those fuckers would never get to spend.

Greedy bastards.

"We'll take this into the loading dock and lock it up at home. See you there," Sola said to Marcus, then climbed into the driver's side without stopping to make sure Knox was okay. They didn't have time to screw around, and he didn't blame them for not wasting precious seconds on him.

He was one man. They could save thousands. Because damn that concoction was incredible. Irresistible. And there was more not far from him. He licked his lips.

"Shit!" Marcus bellowed as he reached up and slammed the rear rolling door of the truck closed, severing Knox's line of sight with the pile of drugs.

He punched himself, irate that he could be enjoying and coveting the very thing that had ruined any last hope of building a future for himself that didn't involve madness, addiction, and destroying the hopes of who-knew-how-many people.

Knox tried to extract the truck keys from his pocket but couldn't get his fingers to function correctly.

"Buddy, you can't drive like that." Marcus levered him up. Besides, that's not even the right truck. I have the keys for the one they brought." He was kind, speaking slowly and quietly, even though Knox could see the strain at the corners of his eyes.

Kennedy's anguished cries reverberated in Knox's mind, either because they were real or because he was imagining how disappointed she was going to be in him, he wasn't sure. Knox swiped at his ear until his comm popped off. But that didn't stop the wailing. Maybe it was his own, echoing through his mind.

Or was it Riggs's ghost? Or a flashback to the sounds Knox himself had made when he'd woken up and realized his boyfriend was gone?

"Fuck! Fuck!" He yanked on his hair. "Make it stop! Marcus. Please. Make it stop."

"Kennedy will do her best. We need to get to her as

quick as possible." Marcus reached for Knox, but he batted the other man's hands away.

"No! She can't see me like this. She'll hate me."

"She won't." Marcus practically mummified Knox as he pinned his arms to his sides with a bear hug so he couldn't land a swing. "She loves you."

That was all he could take. Knox broke. A primal sound—part rage, part grief, part agony—ripped from him and echoed through the night.

"I've got you." Marcus lifted Knox over his shoulder and all Knox could do was flop there as Marcus carried him to the passenger seat of the truck. His whole body buzzed and freaked out, as if it were a grotesque pinball game, the drugs bouncing around his brain lighting it up. He wanted to run the entire way back to Shields and promise Kennedy it would never happen again. But he couldn't stand the thought of facing her. Of seeing revulsion in her beautiful blue eyes.

"I fucked up. I couldn't think of another way." Knox was shaking too hard to wipe the frothy drool from the corner of his mouth. He clung to Marcus. "Why do I like this? Why do I need it? She's going to hate me. I'm fucking disgusting."

"Nah, she's terrified. Would she be so scared if she despised you?" Marcus settled him into the passenger seat and put the seatbelt around him as if he were a child. He did it with fast, efficient motions far different from a dad out for a leisurely drive, though. "She's on the comms still. She's waiting for us at home. She's got some Narcan, and you didn't do that much. Hopefully, that's going to help neutralize the worst of this shit, okay?"

As he rushed around the other side of the truck, Knox

thought he heard Marcus shout, "Why the fuck didn't we bring some with us?"

It was hard to tell through the mush his brains were turning into.

Marcus climbed into the driver's seat and slammed the door, his breathing ragged.

"Let it kill me. 'Cause she's never going to trust me again." Knox's head hit the window as it lolled. His heart felt like it might burst at any second. "And I don't fucking blame her. Who would want a person like this when she's already got you? You're perfect. I can't do anything right."

Marcus didn't seem to disagree since he quit arguing. Instead he revved the engine, then squealed the tires as he raced out of the lot.

Knox wasn't sure if he was going to cry, be sick, or pass out. He stared up at the moon, wobbling in his double vision, before letting the drugs obscure the nightmare he was living through. For the first time in his life, he didn't enjoy being high. He hated every second of the necessary evil. Whatever he'd done, he'd done it to keep Kennedy and as many other people, even ones he'd never know, safe.

If he survived, that would be cold comfort because the woman he'd always loved would look at him with the disgust he'd earned. And the man who obviously adored her, would let Knox go to keep her. Knox wouldn't blame Marcus. He obviously desired Kennedy as badly as Knox had craved this twisted rush once.

Knox closed his eyes and prayed for an easy out—a painless end to his insurmountable problems. How much could one heart take before it broke completely and shuddered to a stop?

16

Kennedy hovered over Marcus's bed, counting the steady breaths Knox took for several minutes. They were still shallow but not scarily slow anymore.

"You told me he's going to be okay." Marcus frowned. "Were you only saying that to make me feel better?"

"No." She turned and buried her face against his chest, loving how his arms automatically went around her, sheltering her. "His vitals are perfect. He's just sleeping it off now."

"So stop worrying." Marcus ran his fingers through her hair from her temple to her ribs, tucking it behind her ear to get it off her face.

"There's a lot left to be scared of." Kennedy thought about where they would go from here, individually and possibly together.

"Come on, let's sit with the guys. Maybe talking to them will help."

Kennedy bit her lip, then nodded, letting Marcus guide her into his living room where Gavyn, the owner of the Hot Rides motorcycle shop, was sprawled in a leather recliner cattycorner from Roman, who had one booted ankle resting on his opposite knee. Both men wore black jeans, faded T-shirts, and possessed an assortment of chains and tattoos between them.

"Same?" Roman asked.

Kennedy rubbed her scalp, trying to erase her headache. "Yeah."

Marcus sank onto the couch then gathered her into his lap, her back facing his chest, and dusted her hands aside to take over massaging for her. His fingers felt incredible easing the tension from her bit by bit.

"You might have to be prepared to give him some space." Roman winced. "When I OD'd and woke up in the hospital, it was both the best and worst sight to see Carver right there at my bedside."

"How so?" She would have figured having the man he later married by his side would have been a relief.

"Because although he'd never say so, I knew I'd let him down." Roman closed his eyes briefly.

"Yeah. I don't even remember the morning they dragged me out of the pond at Bare Natural after my bender on the Powertools' wedding night, but I'll never forget how much it hurt Amber." Gavyn groaned. "Even after all this time, it doesn't get easier and there's nothing we can do about that."

"Except give ourselves some grace, which in itself is a tough lesson." Roman shot Kennedy a sympathetic stare. "It's going to take time."

She nodded.

"How are you two feeling about what happened?" Gavyn wondered.

"I hate that I couldn't stop it. And that I stood by and

watched him do it instead of me." Marcus's hands trembled on Kennedy's skin, so she angled toward him and kissed him gently, trying to soothe his regrets. It still felt new but entirely right to be able to do that.

"In his shoes, there's no way I would have let you touch it." Roman looked at Marcus like he was nuts.

"Me either." Gavyn shook his head. "It's better that you never know what it's like."

"I'm afraid that this is going to set him back and make it harder for him to change in the ways he was hoping to." Kennedy rested her head on Marcus's shoulder and tried not to rub up against him when he caressed her back.

"You can tell me to shut the fuck up if I'm prying, but I'm assuming that what James told us about the three of you spending some quality time together wasn't about having a fling that day?" Roman was direct but not unkind. Everyone knew he had a dominant streak a mile wide.

"Let's be honest." Kennedy peered up at Marcus, who was smiling at her. This wasn't news to him. "I never got over Knox in the first place. And I've been stupid to let that impact my relationship with Marcus. If Knox is brave enough to admit when he's fucked up, I should be too. Yeah, I want them both and I plan to do whatever I can to make it work."

Gavyn and Roman both grinned as if they'd pulled off a grand prank by getting her to admit what seemed obvious to anyone who knew them well. When she canted her head to one side, Roman jerked his chin toward the bedroom doorway, where Knox stood in the shadows, clutching the door frame as he gaped at her.

"Even now. Seriously? How can that be?" Knox sounded like he'd swallowed a handful of the gravel

Marcus had kicked up when he peeled out of that shitty parking lot earlier.

Kennedy sprang to her feet and rushed toward him. She only slowed, stopping prior to flinging herself at him and smothering him in kisses when she remembered what Gavyn and Roman had recently cautioned. Knox might not believe her when she told him the truth, though maybe having heard it from her when she had been unaware he was listening might help move things along. "Because I have faith in you. It was a horrible situation. Let me get you some water. How do you feel?"

"Like shit." His eyes were barely open, as if the lights were stabbing into his brain. Marcus dimmed them, the darkness outside becoming more apparent.

"How long was I out?" Instead of sitting beside them, Knox wandered to the floor to ceiling windows, surveying Middletown laid out before them.

"About five hours. It's almost dawn," Kennedy told him.

He squinted as he stared down into the parking lot. "Am I still seeing things or is that Liam, Sola, Legend, and Tavish carrying bundles suspiciously shaped like those delivery motherfuckers out to a black truck?"

"Let's not discuss that in front of our company." Marcus hit the switch for the automatic shades, which obscured the obsidian sky and the darker deeds going on down below.

"Trust me, I already know not to mess with the Shields." Roman grinned.

Kennedy crossed to Knox and laid her hand on his shoulder, pressing lightly until he turned. He accepted the glass of water she offered and downed it in a few gulps. She set it aside then paused, wondering if she should hug him. He stepped back, bumping into the window covering.

Score a point for the mechanics.

"Come sit. I'm sure you're exhausted. Your body has been through a lot." She tried not to think too much of the readings she'd taken when Marcus had first delivered Knox to her. If they hadn't at least taken the edge off with the Narcan she'd administered, she didn't want to think about what might have happened.

"Honestly, I'm not tired." Knox took the hand she offered and let her tug him toward the couch where he sat between her and Marcus, perched on the edge. "I feel..."

"Like you want to run, right? But there's nowhere to go." Gavyn suggested.

Knox nodded then winced. "How did you know?"

Gavyn waved. "Because I'm a recovering addict. My name is Gavyn. I'm also the brother of one of James's Powertools ladies, Kayla, and married to one of the Hot Rods wives' sisters."

"I really hope you don't expect me to remember all that." Knox hung his head.

Roman snorted and said, "I'll keep it simple then. I'm Roman, one of the Hot Rods. Gavyn and I met in rehab."

"At least you were smart enough to never have to go back after that." Gavyn winced. "I needed another trip through the system to get it right."

"How long have you two been sober?" Knox wondered.

"Ten years for me. Nine for him." Roman leaned forward, planting his elbows on his knees and clasping his hands. "It's possible to beat this. Only if you stand and fight, though. Running from help and resources won't change it and it won't fix it either."

Knox looked away and swallowed hard. "Right this instant, I can honestly say I have no desire to ever put that junk in my body ever again. I just don't know how I'm going to feel tomorrow or the next time I land in a situation like the one earlier tonight."

"That's never going to happen again." Marcus stared over Kennedy's head, his gaze locking with Knox's. "I'm sorry I didn't get you out of it somehow."

"There wasn't any other way." Knox did reach out then, smothering Kennedy as he encircled both her and Marcus in a giant, if shaky, hug. "I'm so sorry I let you both down."

"You didn't. I swear." Kennedy clung to him, finally having faith things might be okay like Gavyn and Roman had been promising them it would be. "The only way I'd be disappointed is if you let this setback divert you from the path you were already on."

"You're surrounded by people who want nothing more than for you to succeed and believe that you can," Gavyn told Knox. "Try to make it through tonight. Then tomorrow. Don't think further ahead than that."

"Eventually, you'll look back and think...damn, that's a lot of days. If I've come this far, I can keep going." Roman nodded his agreement.

Kennedy hoped Knox took as much solace in their advice as she did. Some of the dread and fear chilling her to the core began to seep from her, replaced by hope.

"Thanks, guys. I appreciate that and I'll keep it in mind." The lines around Knox's mouth eased a bit and he stopped picking at his ravaged cuticles. "Do you think we could have some privacy now?"

"Of course," Gavyn said as he and Roman stood. They exchanged fist bumps with Knox and Marcus before giving Kennedy hugs and kissing her cheek. It made her grateful, all over again, that she'd found the Shields and a home in Middletown where her mind had been opened to what it truly meant to be a good person and all the different ways people could discover happiness.

As the guys shuffled toward the door, Knox called after them, "Make sure you lock me in and never ever tell me where Jordan put that stash, okay? Just in case."

"Don't worry. It's already out of the building or he wouldn't have invited us in." Roman shrugged. "They look out for us too—the Shields, Powertools, Hot Rods, and Hot Rides gangs. Every last one of them. Just like they will for you. Your guy and girl have our numbers. Put them in your phone. Call us any time, day or night, and we'll be there to talk or hang out or whatever it takes to get you through it. You have help. You're not fighting this on your own."

"Thank you." Knox blinked a few times as if he couldn't even process having that kind of unconditional support. What if someone had given him that when he was a kid—family or even her? Things could have turned out so differently.

Kennedy might have beat herself up about it, but she hadn't been grown then either.

All she could do was fix right now.

17

Knox heard the click of the front door shutting. It meant he was alone, ready as he'd ever be to face Marcus and Kennedy and beg their forgiveness. The thought skipping repeatedly through his brain was that he had to find a way to show them he was serious about trying to become the kind of person they both already were—beautiful, generous, worthy of love.

"I'm so sorry," he repeated.

"You don't need to say that again, okay?" Kennedy reached up and cupped his cheeks in her hands. She guided his face to hers for an achingly gentle kiss. "I know you are. It's just that..."

"What?" he asked. Her silence guaranteed not everything was smoothed over yet.

Marcus stood beside them, observing their exchange without interrupting.

"I'm scared," she whispered.

Knox gripped her forearms a little too hard, horrified that he frightened her. He might have left faint bruises if Marcus hadn't been there to peel his hands from her. But even he didn't shove Knox away. Instead, he gathered Knox to him and held him tight, as if that would stop his shuddering.

"Come on." Marcus slid his hands to Knox's ass and lifted, walking them into his bedroom and settling Knox on the bed. This time they didn't leave him alone—they joined him.

Much better.

Kennedy snuggled up to one side of him while Marcus bracketed him on the other. She cupped his shoulder, then propped her chin on top of her hand. "I didn't mean to hurt your feelings, but I think it's important to be honest."

"Yeah. You should be." Knox winced. "I can take it. I deserve it."

"No one's trying to punish you," Marcus said. "There's a lot to unpack. Things are complicated as fuck right now. Hell, last week I didn't even know I was in the market for a boyfriend, and then you turned up. I admit it, I was jealous as fuck."

"Of me? Don't be dumb." Knox rolled his eyes. "You could be on the cover of a magazine. You're in amazing shape, have a job that pays like a zillion dollars a year and lets you act like a fucking superhero—saving the planet, even if no one knows it. Plus...you have Kennedy."

"I didn't. Not until you came." Marcus tipped Knox's face toward him. "Were you listening to James yesterday? You're a part of Kennedy. Without you, she wasn't whole. She wasn't able to give herself to me, because you still had her heart."

"And *that's* why I'm afraid," Kennedy whispered, her eyes shimmering. If she cried because of him, so help him, Knox wouldn't be able to forgive himself. "I can see how things might be. And I'm petrified we won't be able to get our shit together."

"I'm going to do my best for you both." Knox looked up at the two people who were capable of pulling him out of the hole he'd dug for himself and, by some miracle, willing to do it, too.

"That's all we can ask." Kennedy kissed a path along his chin to his lips, then sipped from them for a while before letting Marcus have a turn.

"You were incredible earlier. You got us the break we needed and kept that stuff from getting sold to unsuspecting people." Marcus wasn't quite as careful with him as Kennedy had been, and Knox didn't mind in the least.

"I guess we make a good team." Knox couldn't deny they'd partnered perfectly. All things considered, everyone had come out alive. That alone was a miracle.

Kennedy and Marcus loved on him, caressing his chest and nuzzling his neck until things started to get steamier than simple comforting touches dictated. Knox cleared his throat. "I doubt I can get it up right now. But that doesn't mean I don't want to watch you two enjoying yourselves. I'm sure you're riding the wave of adrenaline still."

Marcus and Kennedy exchanged a smoldering stare over his torso. Neither one denied it. Instead they inched closer and closer as if they were two magnets being drawn inevitably together. When they kissed, the exchange brimmed with passion and the urgency brought on by residual despair and horror.

Knox let himself float in a world where he hadn't died and the two people he had fallen hard for didn't hate him.

He relaxed as they made out, graduating from sweet exchanges to something hungry and impatient.

After all the time they'd spent so close and yet refusing to explore their attraction, he didn't blame them for letting their emotions boil over now. Marcus stood on the bed, making it dip. He ripped his shirt over his head, then unbuckled his jeans and when they pooled at his feet on the mattress, Knox ran his hand along one of Marcus's chiseled calves, impressed that he could barely get his hand halfway around the widest part. Marcus was powerful and possessed enough self-control for the three of them.

He'd honed his body into near-perfection and had somehow kept his hands off Kennedy until she was ready to explore what was between them. He was a far better man than Knox could ever attempt to be. When he realized Knox and Kennedy were both spellbound, staring at his bared form, his cock twitched. "Why am I the only one naked?"

Knox's entire outfit consisted of a pair of the cotton gym shorts James had bought for him along with a few other wardrobe essentials. The man had a good eye, Knox would give him that. Most everything had fit and been comfy, casual gear. And the few dressier outfits seemed like they might actually look decent on him, although he'd never had a reason for clothes like that before.

When Kennedy smiled coyly at Marcus and started swaying as she stripped her scrub top off, followed shortly by her yoga pants, Knox figured what the hell? He peeled his shorts off and tossed them onto the floor.

"Much better." Marcus settled onto the bed again, this time drawing Kennedy to him.

"Hey, watch where you're putting those knees!" Knox cupped his junk as Kennedy ended up between his legs.

"They're right where I want them," Marcus practically growled, going bossy and possessive in a way Knox hadn't seen from him yet, though he couldn't say he disliked it. "I have an idea."

Marcus spun Kennedy to face Knox as she knelt between his thighs. Marcus came up behind her, cupping her breasts. The contrast of his dark hands on her pale skin was beautiful to Knox. How could he like two people who were so different and yet had so much in common?

Kennedy's head tipped onto Marcus's shoulder, exposing her neck. He gently wrapped his hand around the long column and dipped her forward so that her tit was right in front of Knox's face. Knox didn't need any more instruction than that. He feasted on the offering Marcus made of her body, laving her nipple with the flat of his tongue before suckling until she mewled.

"You like that?" Marcus asked, although the answer was plain.

"Yeah." She gasped when Knox bit lightly.

"Good. He's going to take care of you while I fuck you." Marcus slapped her ass, then placed her in Knox's arms. The fact that he trusted Knox to tend to her meant more than he could say.

He wasn't about to disappoint either of them again that night.

Knox strained upward until he sealed his mouth over hers. They glided over each other's parted lips as she sighed and he concentrated on doing whatever she seemed to enjoy most.

It was around the moment that his hand wandered down her belly and rubbed her mound that Marcus groaned. Knox looked up and caught the other man stroking his impressive cock as he watched them kissing.

Kennedy glanced over her shoulder, shoved her ass in the air, and teased Marcus. "Planning to do something with that thing?"

"Only if you ask me nicely." Marcus was a bad liar. He was putting his dick in her in ten seconds or less. But she didn't delay the inevitable.

"Please, Marcus. Fuck me while Knox holds me." She resumed kissing him, knowing full well that Marcus was going to give her exactly what she wanted.

Marcus shuffled behind her on his knees and slapped his dick against her ass a couple times before aligning himself with her pussy. Knox knew the instant he'd fused them, because Kennedy tensed in his hold. Knox redoubled his efforts, sucking on her tongue and kneading her breasts to distract her from any initial discomfort as Marcus stretched her around his thick hard-on.

"Damn, you feel so good on me." Marcus groaned.

Knox could relate. Even if all he was doing was caressing Kennedy, she brought him more pleasure than he could have imagined. Sharing this with them made him feel like the luckiest bastard alive, which he probably was by this point.

When Marcus grabbed her hips and began to ride, Knox switched his tactic. He trailed his hand across her taut stomach and down to her pussy. First he circled his finger around Marcus's dick, embedded within her, gathering up some of the natural lubrication he'd already elicited from her.

Then Knox used it to swirl his thumb around her clit. He remembered how she enjoyed a light, indirect pressure from the times they'd fooled around as teenagers.

"Oh shit." Her eyes flew wide and her jaw hung open as she was caught between him and Marcus, both of them intent on giving her as much pleasure as she could stand.

"Fuck, she's hugging my cock already." Marcus leaned forward and bit her shoulder.

Which, combined with Knox's strumming, was all it took to set her off.

Kennedy dug her fingernails into his upper arms as she flew apart around Marcus, who didn't stop plowing into her with an unrelenting series of long, slow plunges. It was a quick and hard release, but ebbed nearly as fast as it had crested.

"That was a nice start," Marcus purred at her.

Kennedy pushed herself up from Knox's chest, careful to avoid his stitches. She didn't proclaim that she couldn't come again or try to evade them. Instead she rocked back on Marcus and tossed her hair like a star. Damn.

"Why don't you sit on my face so I can help you with the next one?" Knox asked, on board with being smothered if that's what it took for her to fly again.

"I have a better idea." Kennedy moved, but instead of climbing up him, she scooted downward.

"I like the way you think." Marcus smacked her ass then fisted his hand in her hair, using the grip to guide her mouth to Knox's dick.

Despite his earlier assumptions, Knox felt his cock start to fill as she drew it into her wet, warm mouth and toyed with him. She licked him from root to tip, then sucked without intent. Not trying to get him off but merely enjoying holding him within her while Marcus continued to rail her. Knox figured she didn't have a lot of experience, maybe only the few times they'd experimented together. But her unpracticed motions were plenty to wake his dick from near-death.

"Does that feel good?" Kennedy pulled off long enough to ask. "Do you like it?"

Knox and Marcus both burst out laughing. In the middle of the hottest moment of his life, they could have fun. It was magical and sealed something in him right then. This was what he wanted. Forever. Love and joy and a whole lot of steam.

"What?" Kennedy got shy and withdrew a bit.

"Oh no, you don't." Marcus put her face back into place, then blanketed her back so that his cheek was right next to hers. "You don't need to be a genius to get a guy off. Of course it feels incredible, I'm sure."

"What he said." Knox could feel Marcus's breath on the base of his cock.

"Here. I'll prove it to you." Marcus ground against Kennedy's ass, joining them as deeply as she could take him.

Knox didn't quite understand what he meant until Marcus opened his mouth and licked around Kennedy's lips. Surprised, she pulled off of Knox's shaft, leaving his rapidly stiffening cock open for Marcus to have a taste.

Kennedy and Marcus kept fucking while they took turns sucking Knox. He'd never seen anything more alluring in his life than the pair of them going down on him while getting each other off.

"Have you ever done this before?" Knox asked, suspecting the other guy was a BJ virgin, though not because what he was doing was crude.

"Nope. But I've watched a hell of a lot of porn and gotten a few myself." Marcus turned his head to kiss

Kennedy, their lips bouncing off Knox's cock in the process. He murmured to her, "Men are simple creatures. Keep sucking and I'll keep fucking."

Kennedy moaned then devoured Knox, growing bolder as she realized that she wasn't about to hurt him and figured out what he responded to most.

Soon she was bobbing over him as Marcus bottomed out in her, pushing her forward so she took Knox deeper and deeper. Kennedy must have enjoyed sharing him with Marcus as much as Knox enjoyed sharing her with the other man.

Soon she reached between her legs and rubbed her clit. It only took a few seconds before she was quaking between Knox's legs. He withdrew from her mouth so she could breathe through her orgasm and so she didn't accidently bite down on him while she surrendered to the rapture Marcus was giving her.

"How's that?" Marcus asked her, still filling her pulsing pussy.

"Better, but..." She turned her head and nipped Knox's hip. "Now I want him too."

"Looks like he's plenty hard enough to give me a break." Marcus lifted her off his dick, which glistened in the light from the bedside lamp. She'd soaked his shaft.

Kennedy climbed Knox. He was grateful they didn't need him to do much because while his cock might be willing, the rest of him was still pretty beat up. She straddled him, lifting his cock until she could slide down it. When she sat on him, holding him fully within her, he clutched the bed sheets. He didn't want to embarrass himself and come before she'd even started moving but she felt like everything he'd ever been too scared to hope for—coming home, understanding, and perfect chemistry.

Marcus edged closer to look over her shoulder at where they were joined. The guy hadn't even come yet. He had to be craving more.

Kennedy glanced back at him and said, "I want you both."

Marcus grimaced. "I'm not sure you can take me in the ass without it hurting. Not without prep."

"I didn't say anything about my ass." Kennedy spread her legs, making more room for Marcus to maneuver. "I want both of you inside of me at the same time. In my pussy."

"Uh, is that a good idea?" Knox asked.

"I'm a doctor. It's fine. Trust me." Kennedy nipped his lower lip. "And if we end up in the ER with some kind of freaky sex emergency, I know enough people at the hospital to swear them to secrecy."

Marcus chuckled. "It's not going to come to that. Tell me if this hurts even the slightest bit."

He nudged Knox's balls with the tip of his cock, making Knox groan, then followed the root of Knox's cock upwards, using it to shoehorn his way inside Kennedy.

Though it seemed at first like he wasn't going to be able to wedge himself inside, after a few passes, he began to work deeper and deeper.

Kennedy stretched around them, squeezing their cocks as they slid against each other within her. Marcus made a noise that reverberated his chest against Kennedy's back. Sandwiched between them, she began to tremble.

"You okay?" Knox asked, kissing her forehead, eyelids,

and then the corner of her mouth as he allowed her to breathe through it.

"Incredible," she whispered before shifting her weight so that she was sheathing them, using them both to the best effect.

Kennedy went wild, bucking between them, while grinding her pussy on his abdomen. He could feel her fisting tighter around them as she neared climax. But he wasn't quite ready when she screamed their names and shattered, rippling over them, pressing their cocks together, as she came and came.

"Ah, damn. Okay. Too much." Kennedy shifted until Marcus's cock slipped from within her, but the guy still hadn't lost it. Knox had no idea how he was holding off without the lingering effects of opioids in his system, which Knox blamed for his delayed responses. "Sorry."

Marcus spanked her again. "Don't you dare apologize for the best sex of my life."

Knox couldn't agree more. So he did what he could, and asked for what he craved not only to take the pressure off Kennedy, but because he wanted it for himself. "Fuck me instead."

Marcus froze and looked over at both Knox and Kennedy.

Kennedy groaned. "I thought I was done. Nope. One more."

Knox smiled slow and wide at that. Her pussy clenched around his cock, which was still buried in her. This would work just fine.

"I don't want to hurt you any more than I want to hurt her." Marcus hesitated.

"I'm sure I can handle you if you take it slow." Besides,

he was willing to suffer some if it meant his lovers were satisfied.

Knox rolled to his side, and Marcus respected him enough not to argue anymore. He dove behind Knox, flailing over the side of the bed in search of the lube he'd stashed in the drawer of the bedside table after their escapades with Kennedy's toys.

Knox looked straight into Kennedy's open eyes and swore he could see her soul. "It's a night of firsts."

"What does that mean?" she asked.

"I've never bottomed before. Never had the desire to." He shrugged. "Never had sex with someone I admitted I was in love with either."

Kennedy halted his confessions by kissing him. Maybe she wasn't ready for him to drop the L-bomb. Marcus either. Though the man was gentle when he spread Knox open with a lubed finger, then two. And when Knox was afraid he might lose himself inside Kennedy before Marcus had joined them, he tipped his head up and glanced at Marcus. "Go ahead. Do it."

Marcus fit himself to Knox's ass and pressed inside, burrowing deep enough to keep from being squeezed out again before giving Knox a moment to cope. His eyes flew open, and he clutched Kennedy to him, thrilled to be at the center of their attention and easy affection.

It meant something to him to be held by them. To be impaled on Marcus's cock while entrenched in Kennedy's pussy. Their arms went around him and they held him as they made love to him, showing him with every whisper and caress how glad they were to have him back.

Knox knew in that moment that he was going to be okay. Because there was no way he would ever risk messing this up. He'd found his place in the universe. The spot he'd always been meant for.

It was here, in the arms of two generous lovers and incredible people.

Whether they were ready to accept it or not, he intended to spend the rest of his life showering them with the love they had earned.

Knox kissed Kennedy, pouring his heart into the exchange. And when Marcus began to move, targeting Knox's prostate with eerie precision, Knox knew he wasn't going to last much longer.

"Feels great. You're so tight." Marcus groaned and bit Knox's neck.

That was the thing that broke him. That sensual, possessive gesture. Knox stared into Kennedy's eyes, memorizing the exact shade of blue they were in that instant, like the Caribbean Sea, which he'd only ever seen in ads on TV.

"He's going to come," Kennedy warned Marcus.

"I know. I can feel him clamping around me." Marcus groaned. "Me too. Can't hold back this time."

"Don't you dare," Knox snarled as his balls drew up tight to his body and the first pulse of come shot from his cock.

"I'm with you!" Kennedy cried.

Knox wasn't sure which of them fell first, but within instants they were each writhing and emitting guttural sounds that might have been pain leaving their souls and rapture replacing it. They clung to each other as the intensity of the moment rushed through them, amplifying each other's reactions.

Knox's ass milked Marcus's cock dry even as he flooded Kennedy's pussy with his own release. She drew every last drop from his balls with the rhythmic contractions of her rings of muscles.

And as they lay there, catching their breath then dozing off, still connected, Knox had never felt so secure in his place or sure of his purpose. This wasn't fooling around. It was forever.

As he watched over them sleeping, he swore he would do anything, even become the man they deserved, to ensure he never had to give them up. At least that's what he thought until his phone buzzed on the nightstand and the message he received made it clear that he would never be free to make those sorts of commitments.

Knox spent the rest of the night staring up at the ceiling, trying to think of a way out of the trap he'd been caught in since he was seventeen. Addiction had destroyed him, but if he wasn't careful, he could be the poison that spoiled Marcus and Kennedy's lives.

18

Kennedy stared into the moonless sky. Without the night vision goggles from her kit, she wouldn't have been able to see shit from her outpost. She hunkered down beside Aarav on a hilltop overlooking the edge of the jungle where a massive drug manufacturing complex was mostly obscured by a lush canopy of leaves. Their "guests" had given up the location fairly easily, along with a few key details about the formula of their new superdrug—mostly that only one person had control of it and that it was stashed in his office.

The past forty-eight hours had involved a lot of strategizing, intel gathering, a couple of quickies. What it hadn't included was hardly any sleep other than what she'd managed to steal on the private jet flight James had arranged for her, and most of the rest of the team. Jordan, James, Ace, and Ruby were probably huddled together around the table in the command center, monitoring the feeds from each of the field agents' body cams as well as maintaining the comms, though they were eerily silent at the moment.

Fruit bats circled overhead and monkeys chattered in the distance. Bugs and who knew what else slithered in the shadows, making her edge closer to Aarav while still being mindful of his personal space. She didn't want to risk nudging him at the wrong moment, given the precision necessary to make his long-distance shots.

Kennedy squinted, barely making out a rustle of movement she knew belonged to one of the pairs creeping up on the complex from various angles. Her stare was locked on the pathway she knew Knox and Marcus were taking on their approach.

At first, she'd been surprised Jordan intended for Knox to come along on this assignment, but she recognized that he had more experience with these sorts of shit shows than she'd like to consider, just from the opposite side. He'd run a profitable arm of a drug cartel's operations, and that didn't come without conflict. Besides, Jordan had seemed to think he might have information or connections that could tip things in their favor in the heat of the moment.

Kennedy had to wonder if he was also giving Knox the chance to atone for some of his previous poor decisions. No matter what the reason, she hated that both he and Marcus were out there, crawling toward danger instead of away from it, but that's also what made them men she could love.

Everything seemed to be going according to plan, which was essentially break in, sneak around, hopefully not get caught, find the recipe, and get the hell out before blowing the factory to bits—though no one really believed that was how things would ultimately go down.

There were too many eyes on the entrances and far too many guns patrolling. The rest was going to be an improvisation.

Aarav snapped her from her thoughts when he uttered something in Bengali that sounded a lot like a curse to her.

"What?" Kennedy squinted into the distance.

"Nolan and Sola have been made," Aarav told her at the same time he disclosed the bad news to the rest of the team back in Middletown. "I can start picking off guards to even the odds, but then they'll know we're here. The whole team."

"We don't have a lot of options. They're going to find our people." Jordan's voice was tight. "Go ahead, Aarav. Give them the best advantage you can. Take every clean shot."

Aarav didn't respond verbally. Instead, he pulled the trigger on the stabilized rifle he was stretched out along. The damn thing was nearly as big as he was. He went so still she knew he wasn't breathing and wondered if he could even stop his own heart. He was efficient—shot, reset, another shot...

And James's play by play over the comms made it clear Aarav didn't miss.

He'd gone through at least a dozen rounds when chaos broke out over the lines. Kennedy tapped her goggles so that one eye displayed footage from Marcus's body cam along with the blended audio of her teammates.

Kennedy debated taking up chewing her nails like Knox when she saw Liam and Nolan smashing a window before tucking and rolling through it onto a concrete slab floor. Unfortunately, that was about as far as they got. Sola took out a man rushing her, but then she and the rest of the agents were swarmed and fighting hand to hand. Enemies were everywhere.

Too many.

Aarav groaned. "They're mixed now. I can't target any more without risking one of our own."

"You did your part," Jordan told him. "Sit tight and let's see if we get another chance to help them out."

But from where Kennedy sat, watching in horror, it wasn't looking like most of their other operations. They didn't have the manpower to go up against this much sheer volume. Punches were flying. Kicks, grunts, and curses echoed from both sides, too. Someone grabbed hold of Liam's arm and wrenched, making him howl before he flattened the bastard.

And then, a voice cut through the din. "Knox. Is that you?"

Marcus whipped around to face the newcomer, giving Kennedy a good look at the man dressed in a black suit with slicked-back hair. He wasn't scarred or ugly. No, the man was only about five or ten years older than her and covered with black-and-gray tattoos that would have been sexy if she didn't have an instinctive sense that the man they were decorating was pure evil incarnate.

"Capture, not kill!" the man bellowed.

Several more of his lackeys were taken out by the Shields then. They had the advantage because they were fighting full out despite the reprieve granted by their enemy's directive. But eventually, each of them was outnumbered at least five to one. They were herded together, disarmed one-by-one until they stood in a circle, their backs toward the center, facing out.

"That's better." The man flashed a wicked too-white smile. "Knox. Welcome home."

He strode down an open-backed metal stairway from the catwalk over the cooking floor and approached the Shields. Kennedy knew the first person with an opening would break that bastard's neck.

"What about now, Aarav? Do you have a clear shot?" Jordan asked.

"Negative. There's a steel pillar in the way. The guy isn't an idiot," Aarav hissed.

Instead of telling the asshole to fuck off, Knox tucked his gun into the shoulder holster James had fitted him with and strode over to the drug lord. He bowed his head as he approached. Instead of spitting on the man, Knox took his outstretched hand and kissed his knuckles. "Sorry it took longer than expected, Vex. These guys aren't easy to fool. I had to be careful."

What? No! Kennedy's blood froze in her veins and her lips went numb. She tapped her comms as if she wasn't hearing them correctly and scrubbed her eyes as if it would change what she was seeing as she watched Knox betray each and every one of them. Her entire being vibrated with rage and pain and self-loathing that she hadn't known better.

"I can see that. And our delivery drivers?" Vex asked.

"Sacrifices for the cause." Knox shrugged one shoulder.

"What the fuck is this?" James hissed from the command center.

Jordan shushed him. "Wait and watch. Give him a chance to do the right thing."

"You knew? You knew he was a plant or a double-cross or whatever the fuck this is?" This time it was Ace, and it sounded like he'd jumped up from his chair, allowing it to crash onto the floor. After all, Liam was out there, exposed and vulnerable like Marcus. Kennedy could relate, except she'd fallen for Knox's act. "You're gambling their lives on a man who can't say no to that shit? This is madness!"

Inside the factory, Marcus jerked, reminding Kennedy that the entire team, Knox included, could hear every word they were saying.

Jordan cleared his throat. "I know about the deal you cut, Knox, and how it will get you closer to the heart of this operation than we could have ever managed. You can do something none of the rest of us can. I believe in you."

Kennedy bit her fist to keep from screaming and giving away their location in the jungle. She'd done this. Brought Knox into Shields and put Marcus and the rest of her friends' lives at risk because she vouched for—and slept with—the one man who'd always been able to deceive her. And now he'd even gotten to Jordan, inspiring faith he didn't warrant.

No wonder Jordan had sent Knox with them into the field. She should have known.

"How could you?" she wailed. If she only had a few more seconds to speak to Knox she hoped he could hear her soul ripping apart. "I fucked you. Hell, I *loved* you. How could you be so disloyal not only to me, but to Marcus too? You piece of shit. When your friends kill us all know that I will haunt you for the rest of your days—"

There was no use in saying anything beyond that because Knox ripped the communication device from his ear and smashed it beneath his boot heel on the concrete. For some reason, he left his own camera engaged. Maybe he'd forgotten about it or only cared about shutting her up so he didn't have to feel guilty about screwing them all.

The rest of the Shields in the factory were out of range of Marcus's body camera, but Kennedy was sure none of them were at ease as they had been among friends in the Shields dining hall.

Because of her and her poor judgment—and Knox's uncanny ability to inspire confidence he hadn't earned—they were all going to die.

Without a backward glance, Knox leaned into Vex's one-armed slap on the back, that was as close to a bro-hug as he probably ever got. They turned and walked side-by-side back up the staircase and toward an office at the top.

The metal vats and boilers sitting on the concrete slab of the corrugated warehouse burped out fumes that must be hazardous. Not that the Shields were going to have to worry about the long term effects of that shit.

"What should we do with our company?" one of the drug runners shouted up to Vex.

"Try to keep them from killing you while I have a chat with our boy here and figure out the best way to get rid of them." Vex and Knox laughed as they disappeared into the office.

"Ruby, enlarge Knox's camera feed," Jordan snapped. "Everyone hold. Stay calm. It may not be what it appears."

"It is," Kennedy gasped. "I'm so sorry, everyone. I'm sorry. Marcus—"

She cut off, unable to even speak, the weight of his name and her guilt choking her.

Aarav surprised her by rocking toward her, scooping her up in his muscled arm and sheltering her against his side while still remaining in reach of his rifle. "You couldn't have known, Kennedy. He seemed genuine. And regardless of how this shit warps his judgment, his feelings for you—and Marcus—were obvious."

"It's not enough, is it?" Kennedy sobbed. "It wasn't

then and it's not now. This time Marcus is going to pay for it."

She stared in horror at Aarav, and though she didn't say it, she knew Sola would too. Both of them might endure a nightmare yet tonight.

"Breathe, Kennedy. We'll take things one second at a time. I'm not giving up yet." Aarav squeezed her, shaking her a bit to break her from her shock.

As her disbelief receded, anger took its place. "Maybe I should go in there. I'll wring his neck with my bare hands."

"Sit on her if you have to, Aarav," Jordan commanded. "No one else is going inside that place."

Aarav rolled, pinning her when she would have rushed down the hillside.

"Switch channels, Kennedy. Anyone who can. Watch Knox's feed." Jordan barely breathed the order as if he could hardly stand to speak.

Kennedy did as instructed, though why she cared what that traitor did with the man he'd forsaken them for, she couldn't say. There was a lot of backslapping and a drink poured, though she noticed Knox was too busy talking to take a sip of his.

And when Vex turned and took a sheet of folded paper from a vase in the corner of his office, Knox burst into motion. He used the tumbler in his hand to smash Vex in the base of the skull. The man crumpled. Knox drew his gun and shot the drug lord point-blank in the head.

Jordan didn't cheer, but his grunt sounded satisfied. "That's our boy."

Kennedy froze. Knox snatched the formula from Vex's lifeless hands and held it as if he was staring at it for several heartbeats. He could steal it. Could control the rest of the cartel goons who already knew him and were used to power exchanging hands when someone became more powerful and devious than the previous boss and usurped control.

But what he couldn't do was go rogue and still ensure everyone made it out alive.

Knox paced the office for a second or two, as if trying to formulate a plan. Then he snatched up a lighter from Vex's desk before scribbling something on the back of the formula. He held the paper up, aimed toward his chest so they could read it. *"No other way out. This recipe dies with me. Love you both. RUN"*

Kennedy clawed the ground as Aarav physically restrained her. "No, no, no, no."

"Son of a bitch!" Jordan sounded like he might have punched something.

"He's not going to—" James gasped. "He is."

Jordan bellowed to the rest of the Shields, who were still huddled on the main floor, patiently awaiting instruction as they side-eyed their guards. And when Jordan's orders came, they responded, all at once. "Team, Knox is going to blow a crater in the jungle a mile wide. He's about to set the cooking vats on fire. Get out. Now. All of you. *Go!*"

The drug runners, who vastly outnumbered the Shields, didn't see it coming. All at once, the Shields bolted for the windows they'd come through not that long ago.

At the same time, Knox dropped the burning paper and the lighter off the catwalk. They fell into the air laden with so many fumes it shimmered. The flames didn't even make it halfway to the surface of whatever the hell was bubbling away in the vat below before it went up, initiating a chain reaction.

Aarav released Kennedy and started shooting again, laying cover for the agents sprinting toward the waiting getaway vehicles. He was a high-performance machine, entrancing her with his methodical, lethal, yet somehow beautiful motions. Kennedy scrambled to her feet and bolted, her goggles still showing her the view from Knox's camera, at least until it was completely engulfed in fire and cut out.

She sprinted through the trees, vines whipping her face, chest, arms, and legs.

Kennedy had almost made it to the clearing, prepared to do the only thing she could and give aid to anyone who'd been injured while fleeing, when the night lit up with a flash. It was so big and bright it made the lightning that had destroyed James's car seem like a sparkler compared to Middletown's main fireworks display.

The percussion from the blast sent her sprawling, flying flat onto the ground, stunned for a few seconds before she resumed moving with a crawl before she could start running again, if hunched over. Had anyone survived the impact of that shockwave up close?

Kennedy made it to their cars, and waited, a wall of smoke cutting off her vision. She tapped her comms but nothing worked. A few seconds later, Aarav came up behind her, lugging his gun and scope. His lip was cut and a trail of blood trickled down his chin.

Before she could tend to it, movement registered in her peripheral vision.

Both she and Aarav froze, him drawing a handgun from somewhere and aiming at the flickers.

"Is that your gun or are you just happy to see me?"

Sola asked, the quirk of her sooty brow making it clear that humor was the only way to avoid less productive emotions. There would be plenty of time for panic attacks when they got home.

Behind Sola, the rest of the Shields emerged from the jungle, Nolan limping and Liam favoring his arm. Their clothes were bloodied and charred in places, but as Kennedy counted their heads she realized they were all there. All but one.

"Marcus!" she shouted. "Where is he?"

"I thought he was right behind me." Legend fanned smoke from in front of his face.

"Last I saw, he hesitated." Tavish shook his head. "I think he went back. For Knox."

"There is no Knox." Nolan looked at the new guy like he was an idiot. "Did you feel the fireball that tried to burn its way up our asses?"

Kennedy's eyes grew wide. If there was any chance, any at all, she had to find them. Had to take care of them. They almost certainly would need a medic.

"Oh shit. No." Aarav grabbed for her, but it was too late.

She dodged him and pumped her arms, sprinting into the jungle faster than she'd ever run before. She crashed into things in the dark and ash, careening toward the inferno that raged in the direction the complex used to be in. "Marcus! Marcus!"

Kennedy screamed his name over and over. Her lungs filled with acrid smoke until she was choking on his name. If he hadn't made it out, it didn't matter if she damaged them irreparably. She wouldn't survive the loss of him and Knox both.

"Marcus!" she wailed.

"Why the hell aren't you in the car?" A pissed-off grunt accompanied his chastisement a moment before he broke through a cloud of smoke. "I can't carry you both."

Marcus looked taller and more handsome than she'd ever seen him before as he tromped through the wilderness with Knox hauled over his shoulder. Knox's shirt was gone and his light skin showed plenty of red patches that were guaranteed to blister. But could he still be alive? His entire body was limp, flopping with every step Marcus took.

"Let me see him." She tugged on Marcus's sleeve.

"In the car. We're getting out of here. Now." Marcus didn't stop, he kept moving away from the blaze that was engulfing trees in addition to what was left of the buildings then. Kennedy jogged beside him, grabbing Knox's wrist and feeling for a pulse. It was hard to say for sure given their jostling, but she thought...maybe...there might be something there.

And finally, finally, her own heart began to beat again.

When the three of them entered the clearing, the rest of the Shields sent up a combined roar that seemed almost as loud as the explosion that had ripped through the complex. It was short-lived as they piled into their vehicles and zoomed out of the jungle back to the obscured landing strip where their jet waited.

Kennedy shut off every emotion rioting in her core and focused on keeping Knox alive. Again.

They were an hour into the flight home before she felt comfortable enough to plop onto her ass on the floor of the jet. She stayed nearby the creamy leather sofa where Marcus had laid Knox out, still clutching his hand in hers. The whoosh of the oxygen he was on lulled her.

Marcus joined her, gathering her to him. "You did it, Kennedy. You saved him."

"No, you did." She looked up at him, then rested her head on his shoulder, suddenly too weary to move. "And you saved me too, because I couldn't have lived without him."

"I know." He kissed her disgusting char-scented hair. If he seemed a little sad, he had plenty of reasons for his misery, not the least of which were the heavy things they'd done to shift the scales back into the favor of goodness.

It took a lot out of all of them. Kennedy looked around at the entire team, most of whom had crashed, including Sola, who slumped next to Aarav, her head lolling onto his chest.

Numb and overwhelmed, Kennedy let her own eyes close. There would be time to figure out how the hell to piece the wreckage of their lives back together after they were safe, in Middletown.

"Do you want something for the pain?" Kennedy hesitated before asking as she checked Knox over for at least the seventh time since they'd made it back to Shields headquarters and started the debrief process.

"It's better if I don't." Knox waved off the thought of even legal drugs despite aching in most every part of his body.

"I checked with resources at the hospital and they said that inadequate pain management is also a risk factor for relapse. So if you change your mind before the end of your debrief, have someone come get me. I can also text Gavyn or Roman and ask them to visit if you need them."

"I'm fine, Kennedy." Knox wouldn't have believed himself either, not given his current toasted marshmallow aesthetic. He wondered how long it would take his eyebrows to grow back.

"You two are done." Jordan spoke firmly though kindly to Marcus and Kennedy. "Go on. Get cleaned up, find something to eat, and relax. I'll send your guy up when I'm done with him."

Knox doubted that was going to be how this played out, but he wasn't dumb enough to contradict the head of the Shields. Kennedy glanced back at Knox one last time before Marcus took her elbow and ushered her from the room. Even now, he was still looking out for them like it was some sort of gentlemanly instinct he couldn't turn off.

"Marcus saved my life. I hope he gets a bonus for that," Knox said to Jordan when the door closed behind them.

"Good idea." Jordan turned to James, who was taking notes of the wrap-up interviews. "Take care of that, huh?"

"I'm going to be extra generous if you don't tell me otherwise." James grinned.

From the corner, Ruby chuckled as she clicked away on one of the three laptops perched on her main computer desk. "He can afford it."

"Did you just hack his bank account?" Knox gaped.

"Can't help myself." Ruby cracked her knuckles.

"Have at it, James." Jordan waved away the details, knowing their manager would handle it. Jordan treated his agents like peers, not peons.

Ruby flipped back to one of her other screens, the one with security cameras. "Uh-oh."

"No. No more uh-ohs today." James spun in his chair to stare at her.

Ruby pointed at the feed for Marcus and Kennedy's floor, where Kennedy was disappearing inside her own apartment and Marcus hung his head for a moment, defeated, before entering his own place across the hall. Oh, shit.

"Maybe she just needs some time to decompress. Take

a shower. Whatever." Ruby didn't even sound like she believed her own statement.

"Send Sola to check on her in a bit," Jordan ordered, then focused on Knox. "And you? What are you going to do now? Where are you going to go?"

Knox shrugged. He hadn't thought that far ahead.

"The Vipers are in disarray. Scattered without a clear leader and no one to supply them given their very poor reputation." Jordan nodded. "You did really well back there. Especially by not looking at that formula and making sure it never got on camera. There's no way it survived and not even anyone on our team knows the full thing."

"I didn't trust myself." Knox hated to admit it.

"Well, I do," Jordan was quick to respond. "That's why I'm offering you a job on our team. And a place to stay if you don't end up moving in with Marcus and Kennedy."

"What?" Knox blinked a few times, wondering if the blast had wrecked his hearing.

"I'll kick your ass myself if you ever try to hide something this crucial from me again. However, I get why you felt you had to handle it yourself, and obviously I agreed with you that it was better for the rest of the team not to know in advance so there was no risk of blowing your cover or one of your lovers interfering to protect you. Overall, you've proven yourself to me." Jordan shrugged. "We could use you."

"Oh. Wow. Thanks." Knox would have loved to have finally had a chance to do the work he'd thought he was signing up for all those years ago, when the cops had fucked him over. "But I'm not sure everyone else will be so welcoming."

"For the record..." James adjusted the thick-framed

glasses Knox was pretty sure were purely for style and not improving his eyesight. "Do you believe that because you almost got the entire team killed or because you think things are going to be heavy with Marcus and Kennedy?"

Knox winced. "All of the above. How could any of them trust me? I heard Kennedy's reaction when she thought I was double-crossing you all. She believed it. Immediately."

"Only because she's still wounded from the last time she thought she was wrong about you," Jordan replied.

James hummed before he scrunched his nose. "In my case, I just thought you were a fuckface, sorry. I shouldn't have doubted Jordan. Or you."

"How did you know Vex had contacted me about flipping on the Shields?" Knox narrowed his eyes at Ruby, who finger waved.

"Yeah, she knows everything that comes in and out of the building, communication-wise." Jordan shrugged. "Besides, you gave her your phone the day you told us about your history with the Vipers. Fair warning, she'll probably perv over any dick pics you send Kennedy or Marcus with that thing too."

"Hey! Don't ruin my fun." Ruby threw her hands up.

"Okay, fine, but how did you know I was lying to Vex and not to you guys when I said I'd come back if he cut me in on a bigger percentage of the profits and gave me more turf?" Knox felt like he might be sick repeating that load of bullshit, though Vex had obviously believed it. The man had never understood there were more valuable things in life than drugs, clout, and cash.

"Sometimes you have to trust your gut." Jordan reclined in the chair, tipping it back as he rocked gently. "I see the way you look at Kennedy, and now Marcus too.

There was no way in hell you were going to stab them in the back."

"Do you think there's any way they could believe that after everything that's happened? And could they ever get over all that I've put them through? I don't want to hang around if I'm just going to fuck things up for them," Knox blurted, unsure if he was asking them as colleagues or…as friends.

Ruby raised her hand. "I've got this. Hold, please."

With a few keystrokes, she'd projected a clip onto the giant screen. Based on the angle, it was probably from Marcus's body cam. Knox cringed when he saw himself drop the lighter from the balcony, reliving the moment he was sure he'd signed his own death certificate. But what he hadn't experienced without his comms and as he'd tumbled off the walkway—which had ultimately saved him as it put him right next to the backdoor and the slab of reinforced steel that had protected him from the bulk of the blast—was Kennedy's gut-wrenching wails.

She'd thought he was gone.

When Marcus's feed ended, Ruby swapped it for Aarav's. Kennedy's grief was palpable as seen from the sniper's body cam. It caused Knox to double over and clutch his gut.

"Enough." Jordan flicked his hand at Ruby, who shut the video off.

"That's not the reaction of a woman who hates you," James said quietly. "And Marcus risked his life to go back and look for you when none of us had a speck of hope."

"He hauled me out from under the door and some other shit, which had flipped on top of me. I don't know how it didn't crush me, but I wouldn't have gotten free on my own. The flames were coming and then Marcus was there. I don't remember much after that." Nor did he want to. Knox shuddered.

"They love you, Knox." James tried again. "It might take them a minute to learn to trust you without a doubt. To let those old injuries scab over and to have absolute faith, but the foundation is there. Don't leave and set your relationship back even further."

Knox was more confused than ever. "I see what you're showing me. I do."

In fact, he might never get Kennedy's screams out of his mind.

"It's still tough for me to comprehend, though. Why would two people as fucking decent as them want me?" He stared at Jordan, looking for the slightest twitch in the man's demeanor. "Can you really sit there with a straight face and tell me you didn't assign Marcus to befriend me in order to get as much dirt as possible for this job?"

Jordan grimaced. "Of course that was part of his assignment."

Spy shit was a giant mind fuck. Knox sighed.

"And we all know Kennedy fucked me for the same reason." He shook his head ruefully. "Not that I'm complaining. I'll take what I can get. But now that this is over, maybe we'll find they're not that into me anymore."

"You're so dumb." Ruby let her skull crash into the headrest of her chair as she rolled her eyes dramatically. "Almost as bad as Aarav, I swear."

"He's not stupid, he's lost." James tapped the eraser of his pencil on his planner. "Until you believe that you're worthy of anyone's devotion and desire, nothing we say is going to convince you of how serious Marcus and Kennedy are about you. I just hope you figure it out before it's too late."

"I can't say I'm never going to fuck up again." Knox thought about Gavyn and Roman's numbers in his phone and how he was going to call them the instant he got out of this damn meeting. He could still smell the liquor that had been in the glass he'd smashed on Vex's skull. "Maybe it would be better if I left Marcus and Kennedy alone so they can have something real, something that I don't fuck up."

"I have a better idea," James said. "Take Jordan up on his offer, become one of us. And do something to show your lovers you're committed to them. Not just for a minute, but forever."

"Sure, sounds simple." Knox pinched the bridge of his nose. "How the fuck am I going to do that?"

"I know exactly how." James beamed.

After James explained, and called one of their friends who had the unique skills to make it happen, Knox started to believe too. "Okay. I like it."

"So is that a yes?" Jordan raised a brow and smirked.

"*Hell* yes." Knox knuckled the corner of his eye as everything that had happened and might yet overwhelmed him. This time, in a positive way.

Jordan stood and circled around to Knox. He stuck out his hand and Knox shook it, hoping the other man couldn't feel him trembling. "Welcome to the Shields."

"Thank you. Honestly, all of you saved my life."

"I'm sure you'll have plenty of opportunities to return the favor around here." Jordan patted Knox on the back, saluted James and Ruby, then strolled from the room, whistling. His own husband and wife—Kason and Wren —were probably upstairs, waiting to lift the weight of the stress he bore as the head of their operation from his shoulders.

20

Marcus paced his living room. Why was Knox's debrief taking so fucking long? It had been hours and hours since they'd left him downstairs. At least Kennedy had finally knocked on Marcus's door and asked if she could wait with him after Sola had left her apartment earlier.

They hadn't really talked about anything of consequence and it was driving him insane not knowing where they stood.

"Hey." Kennedy reached out and snagged Marcus's hand on his next lap past where she was curled up on the couch. "Why don't you come sit with me?"

"Because I'm not sure where the lines are right now and I don't think I'll be able to put distance between us if that's what you want."

"Is that what *you* want?" Kennedy tipped her head.

"Of course not. But now that this is over and you have Knox back, I fully understand that you might not need me anymore." Marcus couldn't believe how much lighter he felt when he let that horrible thought escape his heart and fly out of his mouth.

"You can't seriously think that." Kennedy started to laugh, but stopped when she realized he wasn't joining her. "Oh my God, you do."

She stood and put her arms around him, squeezing him tight before going onto her tiptoes to frame his face with her hands. She held it so that he was forced to stare into her eyes when she said, "Marcus, I love you. I have for a long time now. I was just too chicken shit to admit it to either of us."

Then she kissed him slowly, gently, no need to rush or wait until they were so desperate they might explode if they didn't vent some of their longing. This was something peaceful and enduring. Something he would prize having forever.

Kennedy pulled back a hairsbreadth, just enough to whisper, "Apparently, when I fall for someone, I love them for life. So I hope you're okay with that and with the fact that I still want Knox too."

"That makes two of us." Marcus clenched his eyes shut, remembering the instant he'd seen Knox's boot sticking out from behind that reinforced door. He'd been terrified of what he was going to find when he uncovered the other man. They'd gotten so damn lucky.

Kennedy's smile was wide and dazzling. "We'll have to convince Jordan we need him on the team."

"I don't think that'll be very hard." Marcus shook his head and breathed out a faint laugh. "He singlehandedly took out a cartel today, risking his own life to shut it down. But I thought you didn't like the thought of sleeping with your coworkers."

He would quit Shields if he had to, but Marcus hoped

it didn't come to that. What they did might be gruesome, but after that day he was more sure than ever that someone had to do it.

"I think I realized today that being partners on and off the field has its benefits too. We're able to read each other, respond and bring another level of dedication to protecting each other. Knox wasn't the only one saving lives today. You did too."

"You always do." Marcus ran his hand from her shoulders down to her fingers, linking theirs together. "I admire that about you, Kennedy. Even in the midst of destruction, you're putting things back together. Let me be the person who does that for you. And for Knox."

Kennedy took a deep breath and then nodded before looping her arms around his neck and kissing him again, deeper this time.

They might have gotten carried away if there hadn't been a rap on the door right then.

"It's me. Can I come in?" Knox asked.

Marcus made sure Kennedy was steady before he released her and jogged to let Knox inside. He had no shirt on and he was covered in...plastic wrap? "I know you're a snack, but why are you dressed like a sandwich?"

Kennedy cracked up at that, making Marcus's heart soar. Maybe, just maybe, things were going to be okay. Better than.

Knox came into the living room, taking one of each of their hands in his. He squeezed, then said, "Because I wanted both of you to know how fucking serious I am when I say that although I'm sure I don't deserve you, I want you both and I plan to do anything and everything it takes to show you that someday I might figure out how to be the kind of man you can be proud of."

Marcus glanced at Kennedy when her breath hitched, in time to see a single tear track down her porcelain skin. She murmured, "Does that mean you're staying?"

"Well, I hope you don't mind if I do because otherwise, this is going to be a pain in my ass to laser off." Knox turned around then. "It's just the outline. That's all she could do today because of the position of the burns on my back and given how big it is. But it's a start. A jumping off point for more progress. Kind of like me. I wanted both of you to know how serious I am about this. About us."

Marcus couldn't help himself. He stalked forward and wrapped his hand around the front of Knox's throat to hold him in place. Kennedy raced to his side and together they examined the tattoo that covered Knox's entire back. It was easy to see how the massive piece would fully obscure the viper slithering around his spine with a shield. Outlines of decorative elements that would keep it from being a single blob of blackness on his back showed the promise in the piece.

"Blakely did this, didn't she?" Marcus asked.

"Yeah. James hooked me up. I guess the Powertools are working on a studio for her right down the street from here. She's really cool." Knox swallowed hard. "Do you like it?"

"It's perfect." Kennedy placed a kiss on the edge of the protective film. "And I appreciate knowing you're planning on sticking around this time."

"As long as you'll have me, I'm not going anywhere." Knox turned and kissed her before eyeing Marcus. "Is that okay with you?"

Marcus shed his anxieties in an instant. He grinned as he took one each of Knox's and Kennedy's hands then marched into the bedroom, dragging them along with him. Carefully, he helped tip Knox onto the bed, shaking his head. "You've got to quit getting busted up so we can do this properly some time."

Knox laughed at that.

"I'll try my best." He winced and rolled onto his stomach. "I don't think I can handle the bottom today, guys."

"Then why don't you fuck me instead?" Marcus asked.

Knox sputtered. "I...uh...are you sure? 'Cause, yeah, I'd be up for that."

"Obviously." Kennedy smirked. "You don't need a medical degree to diagnose what's happening in your shorts right now."

They laughed, but Knox stayed still, waiting for Marcus to answer him. Marcus shrugged. "Seems fitting. You took Kennedy's virginity. Might as well take mine too."

"Hold on. You've never had someone in your ass before?" Knox sat up then.

Marcus shook his head. "I never imagined this is how my love life would turn out, but I'm not about to argue with the universe when it feels this good."

"We haven't even gotten started yet," Knox promised him.

Kennedy put her hand on Marcus's shoulder and pressed until he joined Knox on the bed as if she was presenting him to her boyfriend. Then she climbed on behind him.

They spent what might have been hours simply holding each other and kissing slowly, their hands wandering over every inch of each other as if to reassure themselves that the three of them were still there and whole. Maybe in a way they never had been before.

Marcus was confident Kennedy had meant what she'd said earlier. That he'd won her heart independently of their new relationship with Knox. She didn't lie and neither did her sighs and moans as the three of them enjoyed each other.

He let himself relax at the center of his two lovers, thrilled that although they'd both claimed he was their rock, they were his sanctuary too. Knox shifted so that he could bury his face in Kennedy's pussy, and when she'd come, he lifted her on top of Marcus so she could slide down his length. Only when they were locked together seamlessly did Marcus wrap her in his arms and roll so that she was tucked beneath him.

He rocked within her as Knox prepared his ass, opening him before easing inside. Marcus's eyes were opened wide, both to an entirely new level of rapture and the freedom that came from not only loving but allowing himself to accept the sometimes messy affection that these two people had for him.

It might not always be perfect, but as long as they were willing to work on it together, he had no doubt that it would last forever.

Unlike him.

They came together slowly, gently, without the frantic edge they'd possessed each time before when they were constantly trying to outrun some hidden enemy that they'd carried within them all along. Marcus felt full, complete, and surrounded by love as he pressed, slid, and ground into Kennedy. He kissed her, caressed her, and promised her the world as Knox did the same to them both.

And when Marcus felt himself losing control, Knox cried out their names.

Marcus's ass tightened on Knox's dick and drew the other man closer to the brink with him.

But it was Kennedy, who went stiff beneath them both then looked up with pure devotion and bliss in her eyes, that triggered both men to fall with her.

She came in rolling waves that sucked Marcus's cock even deeper inside her where he unloaded every drop of his release, flooding her as Knox did the same to his ass. The heat and certainty that washed over the deepest places of his being brought Marcus the most complete satisfaction he'd ever experienced.

And if he was lucky, as it seemed he truly was, he might get to experience that same overpowering love and contentment every night for the rest of his life.

Marcus flipped onto his back and gathered both Knox and Kennedy to his chest. He hugged them as they exchanged a sweet kiss before each of them said at the same time, "I love you."

21

———

Aarav had come to expect the impossible from James. He had a smoking-hot wife who didn't take shit from anyone and a husband who was equally as sexy, plus an entire construction crew worth of lovers whom he shared his spouses with. Keeping the Shields organized seemed like second nature. And he was genuinely a nice guy.

But the man had outdone himself this time.

The Shields' headquarters had been transformed into a classy-as-fuck location for Sevan, Levi, and Ransom's wedding reception. Whereas the photographs Aarav had seen from the previous Powertools weddings at Kayla's original resort, Bare Natural, and even more recent affairs like Ollie, Van, and Kyra's wedding at Hot Rides, had given the impression of homey outdoor events, this one was all about style and class.

This building, at the heart of Middletown, which had been built by James's own hands for Jordan and the Shields, held so many amazing memories already. At least for Aarav, who'd never known what it was like to have somewhere he belonged. A place he referred to as home instead of just where he lived.

Their jobs were hard. They sometimes did terrible things. Saw gruesome parts of humanity that most people were completely oblivious to. They needed occasions like this to offset the others. It was one reason Aarav had stuck around, become part of the team, when he'd only ever operated solo before. A lone wolf who'd finally found his pack.

The polished metal and glass of the Shields headquarters made the perfect backdrop for white flowers and even the crystal chandeliers that had replaced their standard fixtures. The place looked elegant and...hell, he admitted it to himself, romantic.

Or maybe that was just the vibe everyone was giving off around this place lately.

Nolan and Jace twirled Laurel between them in a gorgeous emerald-green gown. Her smile seemed effortless and the remnants of trauma that had haunted her eyes when she first came to town had long been chased away by patient loving from her two boyfriends.

Nearby, the guests of honor were even more striking. Sevan wore a white pantsuit studded with rhinestones that literally made her shine. Around her waist, a long, flowing partial skirt gave the illusion of a formal gown. It was the perfect outfit for a glamorous bride, who also happened to be a kickass motorcycle mechanic who'd once pretended to be a guy to infiltrate and dismantle an infamous MC.

Even the food was over the top, both plentiful and so delicious he had already downed thirds of every appetizer. Aarav thought that if he ever were to be so lucky as to get married, he'd hire James in a second to make the day incredible for him and his mate.

Then again, he'd probably have to have a date first. And that required asking someone out.

Unfortunately, the one person he was interested in had been avoiding him the entire night, as she did more and more often lately. Sola had even started partnering with Liam in the field on some jobs, using Ace's busted arm as an excuse.

The team thought of Aarav as a man without emotion because building a wall between his heart and his trigger finger was what it took for him to get in the zone. It took a lot of brain power to make the mental calculations about distance and wind he needed in order to protect the team he'd come to care too much about.

But the truth was, he'd been struggling lately to keep his emotions in check. Especially around Sola. He leaned against the wall near the dessert station and tried not to be too obvious as he studied her dancing with Kennedy and Ruby. Her long brunette hair was down today, curled, prettier than he'd ever seen it considering she usually opted for a messy bun around headquarters and tight ponytails or braids in the field.

She drew the gazes of every unattached man, and some women, in the place. Even Tom and Ms. Brown— the honorary parents of the Hot Rods and now the rest of their friends too—who whirled nearby, stopped to smile and clap for the dancing women. Kate was bopping on the edge of the dance floor with her husband, Mike, who held their infant while beaming at their older son and daughter partaking in the festivities.

Their daughter, Abby, was of course partying with

Nathan, the two of them joined at the hip—maybe gyrating a little too close for their parents' comfort—now that they were teenagers. Joe and Morgan hung out with Mike and the rest of the Powertools crew, who sat near James, who straddled the space between them and the Shields.

Along with the Hot Rods and Hot Rides, who were intermixed, Aarav spotted Blakely. He admitted it, he was a bit envious of the work she'd done on Knox. Hell, the dude had barely accepted Jordan's job offer and already had a shield permanently inked on his body, nailed down two of their operatives, and made them his for life.

"Do you ever have fun?" Marcus asked as he snagged a variety of fancy cheeses from the charcuterie board. He could easily have passed for a billionaire at the opening of yet another of his entrepreneurial ventures in his impeccable black tux.

"Who says this isn't enjoyable?" Aarav didn't take his stare from Sola. Couldn't. Damn, she was gorgeous. And brave. And took no shit from anyone. Him included.

Liam snorted as he and Ace joined them, doing some ogling of their own. They were focused on Ruby, who looked both outstanding and nearly unrecognizable from the geek girl he knew in her sequined black dress, which swept the floor. Of course, she was also wearing a circlet that he was pretty sure he'd seen in a *Lord of the Rings* movie, so she hadn't entirely lost her spirit.

"It'd be more fun if you went and joined her," Marcus promised.

"Yeah, then why are you here talking to me instead of spending time with your lovers?" Aarav raised a brow.

"Needed to refuel and bring them some more food too so that we have enough energy for later." Marcus waved at Kennedy, who blew him a kiss. Knox laughed, a real down-to-his-soul laugh, and kissed her cheek. "You know, if you quit screwing around, maybe you could get lucky tonight too."

Aarav thought there was a better chance of him crashing and burning, but maybe it was the pheromones flying around the room giving him bad ideas that encouraged him to listen to his friends for once. "Okay, fine. I'm going to cut in."

Did he even remember how to dance? He'd loved to once.

"Go get her, tiger." Liam clapped him on the back and shoved Aarav a bit in that direction. He was still catching up with his momentum when his slick dress shoe hit the dance floor. Instead of approaching suavely and taking one of her friends' places, Aarav instead bowled all three of them over.

Several people gasped, and Mike and Joe jumped into action from the sidelines, helping right the women, who were cracking up.

"Damn, Aarav," Ruby teased. "You didn't have to actually throw yourself at Sola."

He was still trying to come up with something to say that would smooth things over when another man, one he'd never seen before, approached in a suit, holding a single rose. "Are you all right? I'm sorry I'm late."

Sola looked at Aarav, her head tilted. But when he still didn't speak, she dusted herself off and turned her attention to the newcomer. "Oh, hey, Jake. I'm fine. Is that for me?"

He held the rose out to her sheepishly. "Uh, yeah."

What. The. Fuck. She'd invited a plus-one? A douche-y bastard who hadn't even sprung for an entire bouquet? Sola was going to eat that guy alive. Fuck. Maybe that's what she wanted. And if so, Aarav had been right to stay away.

"Let's get you something to eat." Sola took his elbow and steered him away, giving Aarav one last lingering glance before talking about inane bullshit she couldn't possible give a damn about.

"*I* would never leave a woman waiting like that," Aarav grumbled to no one in particular. In fact, he hadn't realized he'd said it out loud until his teammates called him on the lies he tried to tell himself.

"Aarav, I mean this in the nicest way possible…" Ruby propped a hand on her hip. "Fuck off. You've been keeping her waiting for months and months with no indication that you're ever going to get off your ass and see where that spark between you might lead."

"Huh?" He looked up then, surprised.

"Don't screw tonight up for her when she's finally willing to take a chance on someone else."

"Someone else?" No. That wasn't how things worked between them. They were single. Partners. And they didn't screw around with other people.

It was at that exact moment Aarav realized how foolish he'd been. The reflexive possessive feelings that blew away his unflappable mask proved that he was more than infatuated with Sola, and now he had to make sure he didn't lose his chance to tell her so.

Aarav marched over to Sola and said, "Can I speak to you out in the hall?"

"I'm kind of busy." She angled away from him toward the too-pretty guy who was rambling about the boring and inconsequential business deal he'd been making when he should have been meeting up with Sola. He had no idea that what she did everyday was ten thousand times more important.

"Just a minute." Aarav gritted his teeth. "Please."

"Fine!" Sola whipped around, her hair smacking him for her. Over her shoulder she said to her date, "I'll be right back. Get yourself something to eat."

And when they were alone, the music muted by the closed boardroom-turned-ballroom doors, she snapped, "Are you seriously going to fuck this up for me after screwing with my feelings for months?"

"What?" Aarav hadn't meant to do that.

"I can't decide if you're clueless or heartless." Sola crossed her arms, her cheeks flushing with ire.

"Is everything all right here?" Her date peeked in from the gathering. When he caught the exchange in progress, he winced. "It looks like maybe I'm not welcome. Do you know how many giant dudes in there are glaring at me like I'm trespassing?"

Damn straight. Aarav would have to thank them later. This dweeb was no match for Sola. She deserved far better. Even more than he could ever hope to give her.

Sola blinked at Jake as if she knew it too. Her shoulders slumped, making Aarav even madder. She wasn't the quitting type.

"I'm just...gonna go." Her date edged for the door, then pivoted on his heel and practically ran for it, leaving Sola clutching that sad flower.

"What the hell are you smirking for?" Sola spun around to face him again, this time stalking closer as if she might take a swing at him. "If you had any chance before tonight, you sure as shit don't now. I didn't even get to fuck that guy before you scared him away."

"He probably would have been a two-pump chump anyway."

"Two pumps is better than none," Sola growled. "Whatever. I can take care of myself. I don't need you or any man. I'm plenty by myself."

He'd never meant to make her feel like she wasn't enough for anyone, especially not him.

"Sola...wait. I'm sorry." Aarav reached for her, but when he did, he saw Jordan standing in the shadows.

"Boss." Sola lifted her chin and put on her armor, all hint of her emotions disappearing so thoroughly she might be the one they started calling a robot next if she wasn't careful.

Jordan stepped closer and cleared his throat. "Are you two finished?"

"Never got started." Sola tossed her hair over her shoulder.

"I didn't mean to make a scene," Aarav told their boss, but he wanted Sola to hear it too. "Don't worry. This won't impact our ability to work together."

"Good. Because I need to send you off on an assignment. You're the best person for it, and I want you to take Sola to watch your back." Jordan planted his feet. Given the gray suit and expensive-as-fuck watch he was wearing, he really didn't seem like someone to be messed with.

"Will you brief us in the morning? What time?" Aarav took out his phone to add an appointment to his calendar.

"We don't have the luxury of waiting. You're leaving. Right now." Jordan pointed toward the back door. "Your flight takes off in twenty minutes. Wren is packing you some food to go."

Sola looked down at her gorgeous dress and sighed. "I

should have known I wasn't really meant to be at the ball. Fine. It's not like I'm going to be doing anything better tonight. Give me five to change."

"Thanks." Jordan put his hand on her shoulder and squeezed. "For the record, I'm paying you both double for missing out on the rest of the evening. And who knows... maybe it'll give you some time alone to hash things out."

"Doubt it." Sola took off for the elevators.

"All I'm going to say is this." Jordan stepped closer and met Aarav's gaze directly. "You'd be stupid not to try your best to fix whatever just went sideways between you two. Make the most of the trip alone on the private jet, man."

While Jordan probably hadn't intended to imply that Aarav and Sola should become members of the mile-high club and fuck this tension out of their systems, that thought wouldn't leave Aarav's head as they raced for the regional airport where their ride and details on the case awaited.

In fact, he was pretty sure that the sexy times that ensued on that flight were entirely their boss's fault. But that didn't make it any easier to figure out how to show Sola she meant so much more to him than a quick fuck. Especially when they had a corrupt, wealthy bookmaker and money launderer to eliminate before the pursuit of profits could claim the lives of any more innocents.

To FIND out who it takes to bring Aarav and Sola together, read their story, Brazen.

If you'd like to start at the very beginning with the Powertools Crew, you can download a discounted boxset of the first six books HERE.

Yes, I know it says complete series but I wrote a seventh book more recently and haven't gotten around to updating the boxset yet, sorry!

You can find the seventh Powertools book, More the Merrier, HERE.

They are also featured in four books in the Powertools: The Original Crew Returns series starting with Screwed HERE

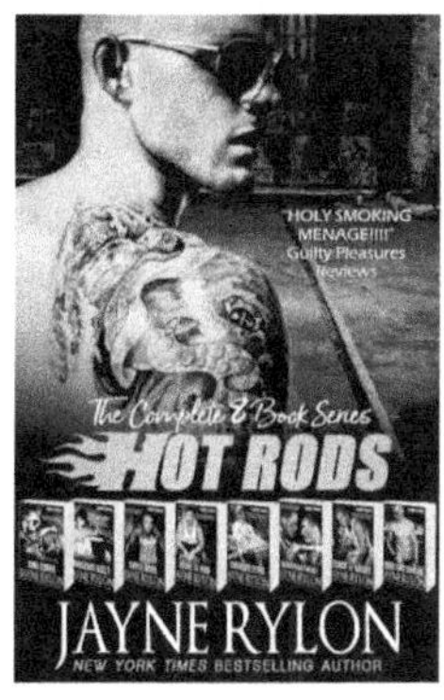

If you missed out on the Powertools: Hot Rods series, you can buy all eight books in a discounted single-volume boxset by clicking HERE.

To read more about the Hot Rides gang, start with Quinn, Trevon, and Devra's story, Wild Ride, click HERE.

Did you know Jayne brought the original Powertools crew back for four more books? Click HERE to get caught up.

CLAIM A $5 GIFT CERTIFICATE

Jayne is so sure you will love her books, she'd like you to try any one of your choosing for free. Claim your $5 gift certificate by signing up for her newsletter. You'll also learn about freebies, new releases, extras, appearances, and more!

www.jaynerylon.com/newsletter

WHAT WAS YOUR FAVORITE PART?

Did you enjoy this book? If so, please leave a review and tell your friends about it. Word of mouth and online reviews are immensely helpful and greatly appreciated.

JAYNE'S SHOP

Check out Jayne's online shop for autographed print books, direct download ebooks, reading-themed apparel up to size 5XL, mugs, tote bags, notebooks, Mr. Rylon's wood (you'll have to see it for yourself!) and more.
www.jaynerylon.com/shop

LISTEN UP!

The majority of Jayne's books are also available in audio format on Audible, Amazon and iTunes.

ABOUT THE AUTHOR

Jayne Rylon is a New York Times and USA Today bestselling author, who has sold more than two million copies of her books. She has received numerous industry awards including the Romantic Times Reviewers' Choice Award for Best Indie Erotic Romance and the Swirl Award, which recognizes excellence in diverse romance. She is an Honor Roll member of the Romance Writers of America. Her stories used to begin as daydreams in seemingly endless business meetings, but now she is a full time author, who employs the skills she learned from her straight-laced corporate existence in the business of writing. She lives in Ohio with her husband, the infamous Mr. Rylon, and kittens they foster for a rescue organization. When she can escape her purple office, she loves to travel the world, avoid speeding tickets in her beloved Sky, SCUBA dive, and–of course–read.

Jayne Loves To Hear From Readers
www.jaynerylon.com
contact@jaynerylon.com
PO Box 10, Pickerington, OH 43147

facebook.com/jaynerylon

twitter.com/JayneRylon

instagram.com/jaynerylon

youtube.com/jaynerylonbooks

bookbub.com/profile/jayne-rylon

amazon.com/author/jaynerylon

ALSO BY JAYNE RYLON

4-EVER

A New Adult Reverse Harem Series

4-Ever Theirs

4-Ever Mine

EVER AFTER DUET

Reverse Harem Featuring Characters From The 4-Ever Series

Fourplay

Fourkeeps

EVER & ALWAYS DUET

Reverse Harem Featuring Characters from the 4-Ever and Ever After Duets

Four Money

Four Love

POWERTOOLS: THE ORIGINAL CREW

Five Guys Who Get It On With Each Other & One Girl. Enough Said?

Kate's Crew

Morgan's Surprise

Kayla's Gift

Devon's Pair

Nailed to the Wall

Hammer it Home

More the Merrier *NEW*

POWERTOOLS: HOT RODS

Powertools Spin Off. Keep up with the Crew plus...

Seven Guys & One Girl. Enough Said?

King Cobra

Mustang Sally

Super Nova

Rebel on the Run

Swinger Style

Barracuda's Heart

Touch of Amber

Long Time Coming

POWERTOOLS: HOT RIDES

Powertools and Hot Rods Spin Off.

Menage and Motorcycles

Wild Ride

Slow Ride

Hard Ride

Joy Ride

Rough Ride

POWERTOOLS: RETURN OF THE CREW

The original crew is back with more steamy menage stories!

Screwed

Drilled

Grind

Pound

POWERTOOLS: THE SHIELDS
Do-gooder Polyamorous Assassins in MMF Menages

Found

Lost

Brazen

Brozen

Claimed

Shared

MEN IN BLUE
Hot Cops Save Women In Danger

Night is Darkest

Razor's Edge

Mistress's Master

Spread Your Wings

Wounded Hearts

Bound For You

DIVEMASTERS
Sexy SCUBA Instructors By Day, Doms On A Mega-Yacht By Night

Going Down

Going Deep

Going Hard

STANDALONE

Menage

Middleman

Nice & Naughty

Contemporary

Where There's Smoke

Report For Booty

COMPASS BROTHERS

Modern Western Family Drama Plus Lots Of Steamy Sex

Northern Exposure

Southern Comfort

Eastern Ambitions

Western Ties

COMPASS GIRLS

Daughters Of The Compass Brothers Drive Their Dads Crazy And Fall In Love

Winter's Thaw

Hope Springs

Summer Fling

Falling Softly

COMPASS BOYS

Sons Of The Compass Brothers Fall In Love

Heaven on Earth

Into the Fire

Still Waters

Light as Air

PLAY DOCTOR

Naughty Sexual Psychology Experiments Anyone?

Dream Machine

Healing Touch

RED LIGHT

A Hooker Who Loves Her Job

Complete Red Light Series Boxset

FREE - Through My Window - FREE

Star

Can't Buy Love

Free For All

PICK YOUR PLEASURES

Choose Your Own Adventure Romances!

Pick Your Pleasure

Pick Your Pleasure 2

RACING FOR LOVE

MMF Menages With Race-Car Driver Heroes

Complete Series Boxset

Driven

Shifting Gears

PARANORMALS

Vampires, Witches, And A Man Trapped In A Painting

Paranormal Double Pack Boxset

Picture Perfect

Reborn

PENTHOUSE PLEASURES

Naughty Manhattanite Neighbors Find Kinky Love

Taboo

Kinky

Sinner

Mentor

ROAMING WITH THE RYLONS

Non-fiction Travelogues about Jayne & Mr. Rylon's Adventures

Australia and New Zealand

www.ingramcontent.com/pod-product-compliance
Lightning Source LLC
Chambersburg PA
CBHW071755190726
48292CB00003B/994